This Book is a work of fiction.

All of the characters, organizations, and events portrayed in the novel are either products of the authors imagination or are used fictitiously. Its not about you.

Copyright 2017 Quick Quill Publishing, LLC

The distribution of this book without permission is a theft of the author's intellectual property. If you would like permission to use material from the book (other than for review purposes), please contact us at www.Quickquillpublishing.com Thank you for your support of the author's rights.

THORNS OF FAE

THESE HALLOWED HILLS SERIES

Quick Quill Publishing

Also by S.L.Mason

DEDICATION

To my niece Felicity.

I have always loved reading to you.

Thank you for listening.

TABLE OF CONTENTS

CHAPTER 1

Little girls want to be a princess, a fairy, or a mermaid. No one wants to be Queen. I certainly didn't. Queens are evil step mothers who spend all their time trying to kill the young beautiful girl—me.

Humming under my breath, I watch the enchantment settle over the rope handrail on the stairs. I'm not walking 700-plus steps just because Deston's a dick.

A rush of wind fills my nostrils as the magic pulls me to the ground floor. Humming again, I reverse the enchantment while planting my feet on the stone floor to study myself. The wound on my leg itches, along with my head and back. Nick was right—it does feel like lice.

The knot in my throat that won't go away forms, and only grows as his voice echoes in my mind. I wish my dad was here. He would say something to help me over it. Something to ease the ache of Nick's loss.

Off in the distance, lower Fae clean the castle, humming the cleaning songs, reminding me of my mother. She hums all the time. The castle could have cleaned itself, but Deston didn't want that either, the dick.

I tear my mind from its wandering journey and force my feet out to the training yard. "You're awake. Are you ready to train?" Janice inquires while standing next to other nameless, faceless Fae, all waiting for me, apparently.

My heart jumps with the timbre of his voice, it's nothing compared to the swooping butterflies in my belly. Who wouldn't get hot and bothered? Janice's jet-black hair hangs down to his mid-back in soft waves, covering muscles honed to kick your ass over a thousand years. And now he was willing to kick mine.

"Yes, and yes," I announce to him, along with all his pretty Fae friends.

Janice began the lesson of the day. "Holding a sword is not like wielding a butter knife or fork. It's a weapon and should be treated with proper respect."

My eyes roll. I don't know how old he assumes I am, or if he actually thinks I'm a moron. But I do know the difference between a sword and a butter knife.

"Can we get past the baby shit?" I ask and pretend to examine my fingernails, over-dramatizing my boredom.

"Sarah," He says with a sigh. "I understand in the human world you learned a thing or two about weapons. But those are your modern-day, projectile-shooting weapons. What I'm about to show you is a classic weapon. One invented by Fae. Somehow humans managed to wield them with a monochrome of proficiency, but they gained no true mastery." He waves his sword around a few times. I'm sure he considered it some kind of flourish. Don't get me wrong, it resembled something from The Last Samurai. "The actual use of it comes nowhere near to the level of proficiency of the Fae. Very rarely does a student surpass its master." He finishes with a thrust and a slash along with a bit of fancy footwork.

I just don't have any interest in waving around a poisonous sword. It isn't poisonous to Fae, only humans, and I don't want to carry it. I don't want to be someone who kills my own kind. Whether I was human anymore or not, deep down I still feel human.

I uncross my arms, I'm telegraphing my irritation and it's not a good idea to tell your enemies exactly what you're feeling or thinking. I'm working on it. Is this how it's gonna be for the rest of my life? Having to carefully orchestrate every move, every facial expression?

"Sarah, are you listening?" Janice asks, sheathing his sword and moving to stand in front of me with both hands on his hips.

Janice's voice pulls me back into my new reality, forcing my participation. I respond. "Sorry, I know I should be listening. I just don't want to kill anybody. And I don't want to get anybody killed. I don't… I don't want to become like you." I bite my lip at my own words, wishing I could chew my tongue off and somehow take them back.

His aura visibly changes, the bright purple fading to pale lilac.

I could kick myself. I rush on, "I'm… I'm, I didn't mean it like that, Janice." I swallow back my apology. "I just meant…

I don't want to be a killer. Fae seemed to kill because they like it." It comes out feeble.

He doesn't turn his back on me, but the cold chill waking off of him is unmistakable. Me and my stupid big mouth.

He continues, "If you're done whining like a Fae-ling, can we begin? I'm not teaching you this so you can become a killer, Sarah. I'm teaching you this so you don't get killed." His aura wakes back as chilly as the cold color it gives off.

"Oh, you mean Fae and the Hallowed Hills aren't done trying to kill me?" One hip cocks to the side with my hand on it, and I raise an eyebrow. *I just can't control my mouth.*

"No, the Fae aren't done trying to kill you and there's a great deal in The Hallowed Hills you've never dreamed of, heard, seen, or could have possibly imagined. And yes, some of it is going to try and kill you. My job is to make sure you survive. Now, are you going to work with me? Or should I just send you into the next challenge unprepared so that you can be slaughtered like all those other girls?" Janice's cutting retort burns my ears.

I hate it when he's right. My hand finds the grip of my sword and it naturally fits my palm as if it was made for only me. Silver slides from its scabbard soundlessly. It is infused with magic to help me wield it. And truthfully, I love the feel of the tang in my hand. It didn't feel like I was holding a sword, but an extension of myself.

Janice's cold instructor voice drones on. "When you wield your weapon, it should feel as if it's a part of you." He raises his blade holding it with two hands to demonstrate.

Check.

"How is it your sword can be wielded with one hand? My dad took me to the Metropolitan Museum in New York. They had swords with different grips. Some were longer than others, and they were specifically listed as single-handed or double-handed swords. Some were so long and large I couldn't imagine anybody waving it around with just one arm. Yet I watch you and you're able to wave your sword with one hand or two hands as you choose." My inquiry is an attempt to lighten the mood.

A dry laugh issues from between his lips. "Why don't you answer your own question? How is it possible that I am capable of wielding a two-handed sword with one hand?" He volleys my query back at me.

I hate the question, with a question answer, but sometimes I'm an idiot. The wake lines coming off of his sword whisper different kinds of magic. Spells layered over spells each imparting a special ability. I'm a moron, why did I ask such a stupid question? "It's enchanted," I say with a half huff.

He turned just enough for me to catch the curve of his cheek hinting at a smile. "Yes, everything in Fae is enchanted. That's why humans have those huge grips they can only wield them one way or the other not both at will. In Fae, swords are crafted to be wielded any way the bearer chooses and still have perfect balance. The grip adjusts to your desire." He turns to face me and flips his sword in the air, letting go before it drifts back down to his waiting hand. "Also, we're not weighed down by the constraints of mass. A sword can be made as light as a bubble and float on air." He slashes at the empty space before him, then sheathes the blade.

"Okay, that's pretty cool. Can you enchant a sword so that it will only go to your hand or always return to your hands when you want, like a boomerang?" I inquire.

He scratches his chin, something he never used to do. The shadow on his otherwise pure, opalescent face is disturbing, almost as if he is growing hair. That's silly, as the only Fae I've ever met with facial hair is Puca. And that's only when he turns into a horse or rabbit or something.

"There was once a song capable of forcing an item to always return to its owner, but I have never heard it and I know of no one who knows it. With your abilities, Sarah, I'm sure you'll be able to figure something out. Shouldn't be too difficult—after all, you seemed to do the impossible quite often these days." He smiles with his full and inviting lips.

I quirk an eyebrow at him, then hitch my mouth to one side. "How comforting to know that you can't help me, but that doesn't mean I can't solve it all on my own. Thanks for nothing, Janice. No offense, but you're supposed to be training me, yet you don't even seem to know half of what I'm asking about." Just when I thought we were going to make nice, nice my mouth gets in the way, again.

He sighs and twirls a strand of hair. "Sarah, the questions you ask, most Fae would never think of. We know what we learned as young Fae-lings. Your questions baffle me. I don't know how to make new magic. All I know is the magic I was taught. I listen to you, you create as you go. It happens without you willing it. It's simply an instinct in use, 'I want this' and your desire makes it happen. I can mimic you but I cannot re-create what you do. I don't know any Fae that can. So, when I tell you I've heard of something, but I don't know how to do it, it's simply because I haven't been taught." He crosses his arms in defense. "It disappeared with time, or perhaps it was something only one Fae knew and never shared with another. We don't create magic, we recreate it — that is our true weakness." He takes a breath and charges on, "It limits us and binds us. We all know the same spells, we can only attack each other the same way. Everything in Fae is old and repetitive. You are the first person I've ever met able to create magic from thin air, never having encountered it before." Janice uncrosses his arms and moves toward me. "All of Fae knows it, and many will try to kill you to stop you from using it. They don't want anyone wielding that kind of power. It frightens them." His brows draw together and his eyes grow dark. "Instead of feeling hope, they feel nothing but fear, anger, and jealousy. So, pick up your sword and learn how to defend yourself, or someone will come along and chop off your head to stop you." The tone of his voice grew cold and desperate. Before I have a chance to reply, he unsheathes his sword and slams it down towards my head.

Without thinking, I immediately hum a bit of Bohemian Rhapsody and a magic shield closes around my crouching form to avoid meeting his blow. His sword crashes against my shield several times.

His eyes widened in shock and pride. "That is what I'm talking about, on instinct alone you protected yourself. There are others that don't want you to do that. They don't want this to happen. They want everything in Fae to continue on as before, with a Queen they're capable of controlling, one who knows nothing more than they know. It's what they understand."

Janice bashes his sword on the flat side against my shield. I lose focus and my shield cracks, allowing the flat of the blade to smack me in the head, shooting stars in every direction.

"You bastard." I leap up to hit him and realize it isn't me hitting him, it's my sword. Silver is in my hand, the sharp edge angled toward him. I watch in horror as I slam the sword down with all my might. Only to clash against the edge of his blade.

"Hate me all you want, Sarah. But if it means you survive, then I did my job and I'll live with your hate for as long as you're Queen." His eyes harden to the deep purple of a stone.

Stepping back, I ask myself. What am I doing? I don't want to kill him. *Why am I so angry?*

"Why do I suddenly hate everything you say?" I scratch at the bumps encircling my head.

Janice's reply is slow and filled with innuendo. "It is not always easy to hear the truth. Sometimes facing it makes your choices difficult. One way or another, you must learn the truth about yourself, your abilities, and all of Fae. You're right, we are evil creatures hiding behind pretty faces. And every one of the pretty faces here, unless you get a sworn allegiance, will do nothing but try to kill you." He moves in closer, lowering his voice. "I guarantee you will not get a sworn allegiance unless you can defeat the best by force. Besting one of us will be difficult, to say the least." He lowers his sword and steps back, sliding it into the waiting scabbard.

"Do you see those two Fae over there?" Janice indicates two males loitering across the courtyard.

I nod my head.

"They're young, I know all Fae look young, but they *are* young. Not much older than you. They're learning to fight with a sword." He extends his arm, pointing to a female Fae whose face holds a long scar from cheek to chin with white hair and poppy-colored eyes. "That is their sword master. Go train with them. Follow the instructions of the swordmaster. I'll be back later to check on you. Do not become distracted by those around you. Some of the Fae here will come to talk or to watch. Focus on what's important. Surviving that is the only thing you need to work on today survival and swordplay." he states.

I nod my head. I said I'd end this. What if killing is what I have to do to end it? *Then that is what I'll do.* I join the other trainees, mimicking their stance. Then, I pull my sword from the scabbard, take up position, and begin the movements.

The swordmaster stares at me with cold eyes and hard-pressed lips. I don't need her approval, only her knowledge.

CHAPTER 2

Days go by before I lay eyes on Janice again. My life settles into a new kind of rhythm. But one look at Janice and the rhythm begins to race along with my heart. His black hair fans out behind him as he strides into the courtyard on a path straight for me. He hands me a coiled rope and a dagger.

Janice's first instructions. "Tie Titom up over there, using only magic."

He indicates one of my fellow students. Titom relaxes his fighting stance and nods his head in acknowledgment to Janice. Then, he presents himself to us. "It is my honor to serve His Grace in any way Deston sees fit." Titom crosses his fingers and arm over his chest and lowers his head.

I shoot Janice a narrow look. Everyone knows I can make up my own magic. The enchanted game zone where Nick died showed them. I purse my lips, sucking in the air to whistle.

Janice cuts me off. "No whistling, no sound, only your desire. What if you can't make a sound, or stealth is necessary?"

Ugh, I hate him. Then, I close my eyes and start to feel the magic around me. The wakes behind me feel off. I turn to face the anomaly, as pain ripples across my face.

Janice's voice slams into me just like his hand. "Keep your eyes open."

Stumbling back, I shift my weight to my bad leg and fall, crashing to the ground and landing on my butt. My eyes are wide open now, and I plant both hands in the dirt next to my aching tail-bone.

"Why didn't you say open your eyes? What the fuck? If you touch me again, I'll… make your clothes burn you for days," I threaten.

He tilts his head back and laughs. "I'll take them off, problem solved." Janice's eyes twinkle with mischief.

My cheeks redden at the thought of him taking his clothes off. Why am I acting like this? No matter what I think, everyone in Fae is beautiful, and I'm not — not anymore. My hand unconsciously lifts toward my face and the scar I know is there, but then stops mid-air.

Janice offers me his hand. Instead, I scoff and push off with my other hand on to the balls of my feet, jumping into a standing position.

Janice laughs out. "Try again, Sarah! Never take your eyes from your opponent and be mindful of the landscape around you. An attack can come from anywhere, even a friend." The double meaning in his words isn't lost on me.

I retort, "I have no friends, and I'm certainly not friends with you." I let the disdain, I didn't feel hang in the air. I was mad he hit me in the head, but it's a long game and I know I have to play it.

I dust my hand on my leather leggings and bend over, and grab the rope and dagger. My irritation fuels the power in my chest. I turn it into magic; the rope creates a slipknot at one end and tightens on the handle of the dagger. At breakneck speed it flies and coils around Titom, crossing over his body up to his neck before pulling him to the ground.

"For my next trick, I shall unravel him." I hum a Bruno Mars song as I spin Titom in the air and dump him in the dirt.

Titom pushes up from the dusty ground, shaking his head. "You don't need to rub my face in it. I'm here at Deston's order to help you train, not to become your plaything," Titom says, seething at me.

The irony of his words isn't lost on me. "Fae don't have a problem turning humans into a plaything—don't like it when the tables are turned, do you?" I laugh under my breath and cross my arms.

He hisses. Now that just makes me want to smash his face in the dirt again. But now isn't the time for a lesson in manners.

"Titom, get up and stop whining! Sarah, try to keep the grime to a minimum." Janice's attempt at diplomacy only spurs me on.

"Funny, I thought Fae didn't mind a fight. I'm only here as Deston's plaything, so why should you be any better? Suck it up, buttercup, let's dance!" My leg itches as the muscle flexes around my wound. I change my stance, dancing on the balls of my feet.

Titom eyes light up to a glowing ember of fiery yellow-orange. His aura wakes change from a glowing orange, to burning fire to match, with muscles coiled he charges me. I pirouette to the side, spinning on my good leg. As he passes, I hum, creating a bubble of jelly, which makes him bounce across the yard. I bend in half, laughing at his body as it topples over with each impact on the ground.

"Sarah, remove the charm. We are working on hand to hand and magic." Janice's voice was laced with amusement. I humpf, then, hum a counter-charm. The bubble pops, splattering jelly-like goo in a puddle of Titom. I hold my belly laughing as Titom squeezes the clear jelly out of his hair.

"You will pay for making a fool of me." His words barely leave his lips before the song starts. The wakes began in his chest, radiating out from there, in a rosie-orange color. The magic wakes race toward me at lightning speed. I brace my good leg behind me and raise my hand.

Calmly I ordered, "Stop!" the magic wake blasts around me. The force pushes my hair back. The wakes had moved around me like water around a stone. I grab the wakes with my hand crushing them like tinfoil. The force of the magic pulls my arm back, so I turn the momentum back on him and watch in fascination as the magic returns to its caster.

The wake smashes into Titom's chest, hurling him back into the stone wall of the castle. His body slumps to the ground.

"Sarah," Janice's voice is laced with horror and concern. "How did you do that?" Janice runs to Titom side, where he checks Titom's vitals while he studies me through his brows. "We're done for today," Janice orders.

Then, he turns his back on me. I'm dismissed. Faltering for a moment, I quickly whirl around and storm out of the courtyard, only to linger in the arched opening of the stairwell.

Lavender appeared and remarks, "My Lady, Titom will be fine, come away. You will give the wrong impression," while pulling gently at my arm.

I turn at Lavender's words and raise an eyebrow. "Wrong impression? What impression is that?" I demand.

"Concern over the injury of a house servant is beneath you." Her reply is quick and to the point.

"You Fae and your class bullshit. I just slammed him into a wall and, yet I'm not supposed to be concerned? How *should* I act?" I retort, with no interest in hearing the reply. I whistle the enchantment on the rope and disappear to the seventh floor and the sanctuary of my rooms.

I didn't intend to hurt Titom, I didn't even know I could throw magic back as a weapon. Janice said magic was dangerous and could rebound —is that what I'd done?

Concern is a human emotion, but my actions resemble Fae more than human. I don't want to become like the Fae. But maybe Deston had been right: over time my human sensibilities will fade away like the Queens of Fae. Will I become one of them? I already look like one.

CHAPTER 3

What would Nick or Arty say? I know what Jake and Tom would say: "Good job! Why didn't you kill him?" But Arty… our friendship seemed so long ago. I saw him only a few days ago, and already the encounter is receding from my mind like an unreal enchantment.

My chest tightens. Nick would have asked how I did it and if I could do it again. He wouldn't have judged. I still see his smile as the life desiccated from his body down to his last remaining green eye.

My fist collides with the side of the wardrobe before me, the sweet sound of wood cracking meets my ears.

The noise doesn't lessen my anger. I slam my foot into the cabinet, again and again, using repetitive motion to stay upright. I plant both feet on the floor, treating the cabinet like a punching bag made of wood. Muscles flexing in my arms and legs don't change the vise grip on my chest squeezing all my air out. My eyes burn to cry but come up dry. I scream at the rhythmic words in my mind, as my right fist pummels the cabinet.

My belly demands food, food I can't keep down. I hum Silver into my hand, her pommel melds for a perfect fit. I swing the sword wide, colliding with the corner, only to slice into the cabinet and cut the door in half while pushing the other door open with the force. I kick the lower fragment of the door until it falls from its frame and clatters to the floor.

"Is this how you treat all your furniture?" Janice inquires as the door clicks closed behind him. Janice stands with both arms crossed and legs wide.

I ignore his question, instead asking one of my own. "So, what's the next one?" I demand.

"What do you mean?" He quirks a brow.

I reply without a glance, "The next challenge. There are four princes, you said there were four challenges, what's the next one?" I hate it when he plays dumb.

Janice slowly supplies. "There are four princes, and there are four challenges. You missed one, and only participated in two." Janice is skirting the question, which irritates me.

"And who's in charge of this one? Jacques went first, Bonn second, so that leaves either Deston or the other guy. Who is in charge of the next challenge?" I demand and wave my arms around, flinging blood from the ripped skin on one hand. It lands on the far wall and sprouts a small blue button-mushroom.

Talking to Janice is like talking to a child. I know he is avoiding the question because it's a simple question.

He interjects, "Jacques was first, Wot second, Bonn third. Deston is in charge of the next and last challenge." Janice's need to be correct did nothing to ease my frustration.

I slam my fist into the wardrobe again and the impact rattles up the length of my arm, causing my shoulder to ache. "Okay, and what will it be?" I exclaim, then wipe the sweat from my forehead.

He responds, "There are parameters, in case you haven't been paying attention. Each challenge follows an element. Earth, fire, and air have all been completed, leaving only water."

I slash at the hanging cabinet door, knocking it from its pathetic hardware. It crashes to the floor with a satisfying bang. Janice shakes his head.

"Water?" I inquire over my shoulder.

"Yes, earth then fire and the last was air." He crouches down and picks up the debris. "Are you finished working out?" he remarks.

I kicked the drawers for good measure. Then, I take out a throwing dagger and begin scraping a bullseye in the remaining door, only to falter at the center. "Wait, the last was air? It didn't seem air like to me. Is that why you've been training me not to use my voice?" I lower the dagger midair and turn to face him.

He responds. "It's not just about not using your voice, Sarah. It's about thinking fast and not relying on what cannot be relied upon. Nothing in Fae is reliable." He hums, and his dagger flies past my face to finish etching the target on the door, only to lodged itself in the center of the bulls-eye, then he continues. "If you rely on Fae to stay the same, you will fail. The one truth is, Fae is always changing, so it will never be what you expect. You expect it to be water, I expect it to be water, but what if it ends up being something else?" His exasperation colors everything—even his aura—orange.

"Well, what else could it be?" I demand. My eyebrows cinch together, pulling on the melted skin on the right side of my face. I don't care what the apothecary said, I could rub all the salve in the world on that scar, it's never going to be soft and supple again. It's always going to be a wrinkled, melted mess.

"Perhaps they'll save water for the final challenge. The challenge no one can control, and instead they'll give you some kind of conglomeration of all the elements," he remarks, then scratches the back of his head.

"Are you sure the third was air?" I cock my eyebrow at him. I can't hear a lie in his words.

He heaves a sigh. "I didn't see the dictate." He shakes his head and crosses his arms while clasping his own chin, as if he was going to stroke facial hair he didn't have.

"The four nymphs said they were looking for the aether to see if I had it," I supply.

"The Elemental Nymphs tested you for the aether in the bubble?" He turns and paces away.

"Yes, isn't that what the challenge was all about?" I ask. Now he really has my attention.

"No. As far as I know, the challenge was not about that at all. I don't think." He shakes his head in frustration.

"Truthfully you have no idea," I snigger with a half-smile.

He paces away from me again, wheels turning in his mind. "And the four nymphs tested you for aether?" he inquires again, which is strange — it's not like Janice to repeat himself.

I retort, "Yeah, I really don't care what happened in the past. The point is I passed. I busted their asses and I made it out. Now I need to figure out what the next test is and win that one too." Alive. "Can we focus on the next one?" Please… *I don't understand why the aether is so important.* I kick the wardrobe again, using my heel this time.

"The only way to know what's to come is to understand the past. The first was earth— everyone knows the maze garden represented earth, soil, the forest. The second was fire, held in a magma cavern." He stops pacing. "People burned to death, you should be thankful you missed that one." He throws his droll, humorless reply over his shoulder then resumes pacing again.

I scoff at him. "You're joking, right? I should be thankful that other people burned to death and not me? That sounds a little self-serving—very Fae, don't you think?" I declare, then scrunch up my lips and shake my head.

Janice cringes away from my retort. He knew what I meant. Surviving, not have participated, means the others, died and the rest hate me. They'd be gunning for me— I need to watch my back. Girls are catty bitches, especially when they all have a common goal: get Sarah. I didn't have to go through the hell they did, and he's telling me I should count my blessings.

I made it out of the forest only because I ran, but Nikki followed, or was it Arty? I shook my head, *don't chase that rabbit down the hole.*

Janice remarks, "My opinion is unchanged. I still believe only water is left and the finale." He runs his fingers through his hair, the black almost reaches his skull now.

"Has Deston asked about your hair?" My query stops Janice in his tracks.

He straightens, but doesn't turn, and his aura takes on the deep amethyst I'd grown to associate with me. Janice replies, "He did. I told him it was to lure out our enemies."

I run the words over in my mind. They weren't a lie, but they lacked truth. Clever. He turns, and I meet his intense stare with one of my own. My heart picks up, and he whirls around to face the window.

"So, it's water or bust?" I announce.

"I'm not sure what bust you're referring to; a bust is a statue of someone's head. Why would it be associated with water?" His questioning response makes me laugh.

I shake my head and walk to the far side of the room, giving myself the space I need to get my emotions under control. He'll either understand and figure it out or not. I don't have time to explain it—after all, I'm sure to him it's considered modern nomenclature. Even though it's a term that's probably hundreds of years old.

To cover the pounding in my chest, I start kicking the cabinet again.

"If you think it's water, then why don't we go for a swim?" I query in an attempt to draw him back to the conversation at hand.

"Human thinking again?" he replies.

I huff at him. How else was I supposed to think? I roll my eyes and cross my arms, but then it strikes me: he's right, I am thinking about it like a human. A human would need to practice swimming. What would a Fae need underwater to survive?

"What would a Fae do if you got trapped underwater?" I stop kicking the cabinet and blow my bangs out of my eyes, then turn to face him full on.

"A better question is, what else is under the water with me?" His reply rang eerie.

Ugh. I stamp my foot. Why does Fae have to be filled with a bunch of bloodthirsty creatures? *Hey, while you're stuck under the water, watch out for the creature from the Black Lagoon?* "What do I need to watch out for in the water?" I huff.

"What do your fairy tales tell you lurks in the ocean depths?" he replies.

Question with a question, touché.

"Well, you could get scary and talk about giant squid. Or we could discuss mermaids, which aren't real, are they?" I shake my head and turn away. I don't want to hear the answer. "We could discuss all range of electric eels and bloodthirsty sharks. There's the Kraken, but that's Greek. What about Nessie the Loch Ness Monster? You're looking for something here, so why don't you give me a clue." I wave my hands around. I hate it when one question turns into twenty.

"Mermaids are real, just not what you think they are, and being as they're Fae, they are exactly what you think, and yes, they do lure men to their deaths. They don't save them," he informs me.

"Great, man-eating mermaids, anything else down there I should know about?" I reply. Check, stay away from the hungry part-human-part-piranha women.

"More than time to list," he remarks.

I gulp. *There's more?*

CHAPTER 4

The list of things that lurk in the dark water was long. I'm sure Janice missed some. Sleep eludes me, and my dreams are filled with bloody water and the sharp teeth of fish. No matter how many times I think I'd awakened to the safety of my room, I realize it's just another dream. By the time my window lightens, my eyes are still heavy with desperately needed sleep.

Lavender prattles around the room in her eternally happy world. It grates on me, and I'm desperate for silence or Nick, Arty, Zoe, a laugh, a friend anyone but a Fae.

Lavender stops insisting on bathing me, and I allow the water from my shower to pour over my face. It's the only way to mask the tears, but the walls tattle and the room ends up being as wet as the tub.

The courtyard holds more Fae than the day before. They set up chairs to watch. I am continually on display, a freak sideshow here for Fae entertainment. My time to heal and train is quickly coming to an end. I'm not ready, though with any luck neither is anyone else. Nikki would be ready. She is a force to be reckoned with— she wants blood even if no one else does.

I brought my sword Silver with me, and the weight of her hanging at my side feels good. I need practice. I missed the burning cave of lava. *The other girls will be out for my blood, won't they? Would I? Maybe?*

"Are you ready to fight?" Janice cuts through the circular conversation in my head, dragging me back to the real world.

I snort. *The real world, right.* "As ready as I will ever be," I reply.

He moves into the fighting stance he'd been drilling into my head. I take the same pose opposite him. He raises his sword for the fight, then takes a luring step toward me.

I remain still, it's bait. Then he paces to the side. I mirror his moves, crossing my feet one in front of the other. He shadow dances with me.

This is boring. He wants me to attack. I allow the rumble in my chest to raise the dust on the ground, forcing it to rise higher with every step. It engulfs our bodies with a waist-high dust cloud. It masks my moves, and his. His aura flames bright yellow and orange. Then, it turns red. I raise my sword to block as the two blades collide. The clang of metal fills the courtyard and rebounds off the walls. I whistle up a bucket from across the yard and fling it at him. He, in turn, sings four rocks to hit me.

I've already played this game, so I hum a bubble around me and listen to the rocks rebound one by one. His eyes grow dark with satisfaction. I hear the whistle and jump, floating to meet him. He leaps up to meet me. I sweep Silver in an arc to rebuff him, but he deflects my blow. I pull a dagger from my bodice and fling it at him. He sings up a magic shield, and the small knives rebound with a loud metallic ring then fall.

The rumble in my chest rises up again, and a dagger lodges itself in his leg.

He yells, "You drew blood, let's break for a moment." Janice pulls the blade from his thigh, and blue blood oozes from the wound. He wipes it on his shirt and hands it back.

"You did well, the dust was a good idea. But lack of visibility works both ways. Don't forget that." Janice's reply is always instructional.

I smile wanly at him. "It was a calculated risk." For once, I didn't lose. I'll take the draw. I turn to survey the crowd— they hadn't clapped or cheered. One woman yawned. *Fucking Fae.*

"Go practice with the others. I'll have this bandaged."

My brows pull together. "I can heal you," I offer.

He freezes, eyes darting around. In a low tone, he replies, "You don't know about Fae healing, remember? I'll see the apothecary." He turns and disappears through an arch on the far side of the courtyard. I stare after him for a minute. Then, I join the other trainees for hand-to-hand sparring.

The motions are relaxing, reminding me of a karate movie. I fight the other trainees and best two out of three, bringing a smile to my face.

"Shall we pick up where we left off?" Janice inquires. He always catches me off guard.

"Sure, wait until I'm tired then show up for the rematch," I reply, smiling.

He looks around the courtyard. "Your playful banter will be misconstrued in this setting," he whispers.

I step back at his rebuff. The fluttering in my belly stills. I was flirting and he shut me down. Burning with shame, I retreat a few steps. The blood that had pooled in my face drains down to my chest and a painful ache. Pulling in air only reinforces the ache. My first instinct is to run away— or scream, I don't know. *I thought he liked me.*

The itch around my head and on my back grows, so I roll my shoulders then my neck to shrugged it off, all the while blinking away the dry burn of humiliation. With one leg behind me and the other slightly pointed in front, I pull Silver from her scabbard. I am ready for a fight.

I close my eyes as the lingering fog appears in the background and mentally push it away. Now was not the time for a fuzzy brain. Opening my eyes, I focus on Janice. He's taken his stance a few feet across from me, armed only with a short sword and a small round buckler. His face is bland, eyes sharp. "You should use a shield." His instructions are meant to help, but I'm not listening. He's made it clear this is business.

"Can you rephrase? I don't want to misconstrue your instruction or actions," I retort, then taunt him with Silver, and shuffle forward only to retreat. His eyes blaze with realization.

"We are sparring, nothing more." His response does nothing to quell my hurt.

I bite down and grind my teeth. *If this is how you want it.* "Come get some, then!" I seethe with the rejection.

Over the course of the last few weeks, I enchanted my equipment and clothes. I need every edge I can get. I'd added enhanced agility and strength, along with increased deflection capabilities. Every item is lighter than air and moving with the speed of light. If magic is about intent, then I intend to win. I wove it into every spell, cloaking myself in what little protections I can conjure. With each day I improve my ability to attack and defend. I've never put it all to the test. Janice won't injure me before the next challenge, and that is my edge.

I attack.

The humming starts in my throat, pulling chairs, carts, posts, and loose wooden debris from all corners of the yard. They crowd around us, swirling like a cyclone. I use the low visibility to dance around a few chairs. Then, I jump from one to the next but Janice has the same idea. I leap from a flying plank to slash at his head, missing by an inch, and watch as clumps of long black-tipped hair drift around in the moving tornado. He disappears in the dusty storm.

My momentary loss of focus cost me. The air in my lungs violently exits my chest, as a foot meets the base of my spine propelling me further into the maelstrom. My shoulder crashes into a wheel. I twist, angling to face the ground, only to meet a new set of blows from a new fighter. Our eyes meet— Titom.

He throws me a wicked grin and slashes at my mid-drift. I crash to the ground and roll. Raising Silver with one hand, I spring to my feet while lashing out at him, only to meet empty air. Humming a protection bubble around me, I change the hurricane debris and add a burning layer to all objects. *Let him walk on that.* Titom slashes at my shield. I snicker at his feeble attempts, then I hum the shield to cover my skin.

Rage wakes from Titom. His rage cuts through all the magic in its path, morphing the very air around him. His eyes roll through the colors of the rainbow, and surrounding him is a thin sheen of magic. The spell wakes inward. The last spell I'd seen do that had been on Brad, but it had emanated from a girth belt. This looked nothing like that.

My fingers lace into the magic coming at me and pull it apart I watch in fascination as it falls to the ground like party streamers. The magic encasing him is so close to his skin I can't reach it without full contact.

He raises his sword, and I only have time to cover my head, protecting it with a bracer. His sword collides with my arm, then the blade cracks and shears off. The tip falls to the ground, lodging in the stone next to my head.

Titom screams in frustration. "I'll kill you, you will never rule Fae!" His eyes bulge with wild hatred. He continues to hack at me. I defect four out of five blows. He's tiring me, wearing me down. I pull a chair out of the swirling air and slam it into his arm, knocking the remnants of the blade from his grasp, then scramble to my feet and crouch over while holding my belly.

Titom picks the chair from the ground with smoking hands and slams it into my side. My bad leg crumples under the abuse and I crash to the flagstones. My head is met with the unforgiving stone, where it bounces off the ground. My sight wavers, and Titom whistles stripping the magic of my shield from me. I tingle with its loss. He grasps a dagger at his waist. The skin on his face pulls tight in a crazed, wicked smile. He grabs the hair, yanking my head back and exposing my neck. "This is how animals should die, in the dirt with their throats cut."

I shake my head to clear the ringing and the fog away but to no avail.

Titom continues for all to hear, "We shouldn't be training them, or teaching them magic. Fae song for Fae, not servants and slaves. I will never be ruled by anything but Wild." He raises his arm. I let the rumble in my chest rise, and the daggers on my bodice pull free of their sheaths, turning his torso into a pin cushion. His arm plunges toward me, but I grab it, angling the blade away from my neck. His grip on my hair loosens.

With all the power I can muster, I pivot, and my foot collides with the side of his knee. He crumples to the ground, pulling me with him. Rolling to my belly, I push up from the ground. A dagger lays at my feet.

"You can't kick a dog and expect it not to bite," I retort, snatching the blade and charge him.

"Sarah, stop! Let Deston bring him justice." Janice's voice cuts through the whirling storm. The feeling floats around in my mind unbidden: *Titom is a threat, kill or be killed is the Fae way.* I bare my teeth and roar.

Titom regains his footing but favors a knee. My lips pull back into a smile. *Good.*

He expects me to stop and take up a position, fight him face to face. That is what Janice has been teaching me. Instead,

I leap through the air as a chair flies around, then faking a step up, I change direction and plow into his side. My body skids over his as we roll, fighting for the dagger. Sweat pours down my face and his. Dirt and grime cake Titom, his breath puffing at me. I end up on top, gripping the hilt. With my other hand on the base, I push down with all my might, grimacing.

"You can't beat the Fae, beast," he huffs his words out.

"I don't need to beat the Fae. Just you dip shit," I growl out. A rumble created from my disdain gives me a burst of energy. The knife slips into his neck, and warm blood bubbles between his lips and sprays from the artery I severed.

His orange eyes widen, and his lips part as if to speak, only to fall slack. His last words never reach my ears, just as his last breath would never reach his lungs.

I pull back, releasing the knife. This isn't what I wanted. *I didn't want to kill anyone.* I sat on Titom's chest, a chest that would never rise or fall again.

Then I scramble off, scooting to the side. My tornado of debris spins, reflecting the chaos raging inside me. My hands are coated in blue blood, mushrooms sprout all around Titom's body and mine. Screaming fills the air and circles me with the storm. His lifeless eyes stare up at me, telling me I did this.

The screaming takes over, seeping into my mind. As I cover my ears, my fingers find the scars and a half-melted stump of an ear. My eyes burn for release of the torrent lurking there.

"Stop! You'll take the castle down," Janice says as he encircles me with his warm arms and pulls me to my feet. Hands cupped my face, forcing me to look in his eyes. "Sarah, stop!" he demands and shakes me.

I look from his lips to his eyes. The deep purple pools implore me to snap out of it. Taking my hand from my stump of an ear, I place it over his heart. The deep purple of his aura lightens to a lilac, moving out from the white of mine. He smiles. "Let the magic rest, let it go," he whispers. I whistle and the raging chaos inside allows the whirling debris to fall where it may.

"I killed him," I mutter. Janice raises my face to meet his, holding my chin in one hand. "Titom killed himself the moment he entered the fight. You defended yourself." His reply was reasonable but wrong.

I shake my head. "No, I humiliated him the other day needlessly. He lashed out. I shouldn't have thrown him in the dirt." The whisper fell from my lips.

The courtyard is a disaster, the Fae crowd cower against the walls, wide-eyed and filthy. Large blocks lay all around, along with cracks running every direction on the curtain wall.

The aching itch around my head increases, as does the stabbing pain in my back. I hunch over with the pain.

Janice steps away from me, his demeanor taking on an all business manner. I spy Deston off in the distance. I guess it's more important to keep up appearances. Deston speaks to a few Fae and heads our way.

The fog descends thicker than before, along with the itching and pain in my back and shoulders. I want to push it away, but I'm incapable of doing so. No matter what I do my mental malaise lingers.

"How is Sarah's training coming along?" Deston addresses Janice as if I wasn't here.

I itch to verbally stab him, but my lips refuse to move. I'm locked inside my mind.

Janice replies, "Excellent, but I think we're done for today." Janice's eyes search my face, then move over to the body, only to return to Deston before giving him a bow with crossed fingers.

Deston surveys the body and the mushrooms growing all around. Then, he turns away to direct his next words at me. "I wish you to come to my rooms." My head nods, and whatever I wanted to say disappears. He takes my hand in his own. The reverence in his touch doesn't make sense. Why did he care? Or did he?

I didn't want to hang out in his rooms alone. The grimy sweat and blood on my skin itches—I want a shower and a good cry.

My eyes focus on his lips. I register he is speaking, but I can't hear the words, a thrill running through me from his touch electrifies my nerve endings. I swallow, and of its own volition, my tongue runs over my lips. Deston stops yammering and a slow smile curves the side of his face.

"You're distracted, Sarah. You seem to have something else on your mind," Deston remarks as he flashes white teeth under the day-glo Fae light, igniting his markings and further mesmerizing my mind.

I shake my head dumbly and reach to scratch the healing stump where my ear should be. The memory of the pain from the acid melting my skin rages back to me. My mind sharpens with the memory of the pain loosening my tongue

My words rush out before the malaise returns. "No, I have this headache that won't go away and I'm tired from training. I didn't expect to kill anyone, and I'd rather take a shower." As an afterthought, I add, "If you'll allow."

His smile widens. He likes docile deference. *Yuk.*

With a smarmy smile, he replies, "I'm glad to hear that you picked up the Fae habit of bathing. The state you were in when you were brought here was atrocious. But the longer you've stayed, the more charming you've become." His pronouncement irritates me.

Physically I warm to his words, though mentally I'm repulsed—overall, its chaos. I want the fire roaring in my veins to die. I didn't like him. He lied about healing me, as well as the competition, the kids Puca was holding, he skipped right over the death part of these challenge's. *Why I'm acting like this?*

Deston leads me to the door of his elevator. "This is where we part ways, my champion. I must oversee my domain and you must rest." His words caress me, and my body responds to the attention. He holds my eyes prisoner. I could only watch in horror as his lips close the space between us.

The tip of my tongue travels over my lips in anticipation of contact. His eyes close, and mine follow suit.

The contact causes electricity to race through my veins. Inside I'm screaming, desperate to push him away. His lips work over mine before sucking my lower lip into his mouth and slowly pulling away.

My heart beats through my chest as my breath gets caught in my throat. I'd felt all of this before for real with someone I like. These feelings were nothing more than a pale reflection. Reflection or not, however, I can't turn them off or push them away. I'm trapped.

He kisses my hand and steps back into the box. The fog drifts away, freeing me as the doors to the elevator close. A scream rips from my throat and all I can do is rub my leather bracer across my lips. I'm desperate to remove the taste of his kiss, but all I do is spread the coppery flavor of Titom's blood as its replacement.

I rush to the stairs and hurry down the passageway to my rooms. I thought I'd felt dirty before he kissed me. The door slams against the wall, I never stop running till I meet the sink. The sound of water splashing over my face fills the room. I gargle until I think my tonsils might come up. None of it can remove the feeling of violation that consumes me.

At least he didn't stick his tongue down my throat.

The acid lava climbs my throat, and I have just enough time to reach the toilet before it exits.

CHAPTER 5

Fae is never what you expect. If you expect fire, you get water. You expect stone, you'll get earth. You think someone's your friend, they'll really end up your foe.

Something about Deston is not right, but I can't put my finger on it. When I'm around him, whatever 'it' is, gets worse. I can't be distracted whether we live or die—we being humanity. Whatever happens, whether I survive or not humanity will forget. Maybe not this generation, but eventually this will all become another fairytale. A new set of myths, dwarfing the Greek gods, or the catalyst of an alien invasion story, catapulting us into space.

Or, worst of all, humanity will simply be so few we will forget what really happened. Left to worry only about survival.

By the time Fae comes around again looking for a new Queen, humanity will have grown again, overtaking the planet and leaving nothing but the stories they tell their children.

I'd read the stories. The older the story, the more fear of a bump in the night. Only the modern stories carried the pretty, fluffy, winged fairy tales I'd gotten.

I'm never going to sleep, so I crawl out of bed and whistle up the mirror. Its ornamental outline is unchanged from a few hours ago, along with the image in it. I still can't resolve myself to the face in front of me. I see it, it's me, but I'm more monster than human. I'm not talking about the scar on the side of my face. No, I hear myself talk, and sometimes it sounds like someone else.

I whistle the mirror away. What's the point of looking in the mirror and longing for something I will never have? It isn't going to solve my problems.

Beauty is only skin deep anyway; ugly goes to the bone. My foot collides with the side of the vanity. I didn't need a vanity anymore, I had nothing to be vain about.

I hum, and the wood in the vanity pops and squeaks, morphing into a love-seat, and the chair turns into a coffee table.

I toyed with Titom. I shouldn't have toyed with him. It was wrong— it was Fae.

It is exactly what I accuse Deston of doing. What made it worse is, I'd mocked him; I shouldn't have done that either. Every day I become more like one of them. The only difference is they're still pretty. On the outside, at least.

I hum until the cushions take proper form, plump and inviting. Then, plopping down, I throw my feet up on the coffee table. My mother always yelled about putting feet up, but she isn't here.

She would never be here.

I snap up and stomp to the wardrobe, yank open the bottom drawer, and pull out Artie's cell phone. Then, I throw myself back on the couch.

I wait for it to power up and quit complaining about the lack of signal. I didn't turn it on to make a phone call. Scrolling through the video gallery, I thrust the earbuds in my ears and pick a video.

I watch as Artie records me, switching the camera around and showing his own smiling face. His glasses reflect the shape of his phone, then I listen to the two of us laugh. He's talking about some concert we were supposed to go to, months ago. It's another lifetime and another me. Listening to his voice and seeing his face comforts me. The darkness closes in and I let sleep overwhelm me.

My rinse and repeat day start's again, the only thing different about today from yesterday, yesterday was practice, today is for real. My stomach clenches as whistling from Lavender in the next room reminds me of where I am and what must be done.

"My lady, I must prepare you," she calls in her sing-song voice.

The earbuds fell out of my ear sometime during the night. The battery reads 20%. *Crap I wasted it.* There's no Fae recharge station down here. I take one last look at Artie's face and turn it off.

"That man whose picture you look at on your little box. Who is he?" She is still making the bed and plumping pillows, but I could tell she is intruding, being nosy.

"Just someone I used to know." My reply is dry and emotionless.

"Well that person you used to know is very handsome for a human," she replies. She's just being nice—they don't find humans handsome or pretty. They only find themselves handsome and pretty. "My lady, today is the day. I'm sure you will be magnificently triumphant besting all the other humans." Her declaration is heartfelt.

"If by besting humans you mean killing, thanks, I'm good. Can we not talk about this?" I mutter.

She cringes and busies herself with her work.

I'm thankful, all I want is peace and quiet. There is nothing anyone could say that is going to make me feel better about today.

Lavender dresses me similar to what I'd worn in the enchanted bubble, then leads me to the stairwell like a lamb to the slaughter. The courtyard goes deathly still with my presence. Everyone is holding their breath in anticipation

"So glad you could finally join us. We're off to one of my estates," Deston announces with a little giggle.

I raise an eyebrow and turn to glare at Deston's face.

"Are you the prince in charge of this challenge?" I inquire

"Yes, I am, and I'm very excited." He claps his hands together with glee.

The fog that's been plaguing me surrounds me again, engulfing my mind. The questions I want answered won't come to the surface. I can't get my lips and mind to work in unison. The moment his hand touches my skin, all the pent-up energy I stored for the day drains away, like a bathtub being emptied.

"Your Grace, your carriage awaits." Janice proffers his arm, indicating Deston's carriage. The moment Deston's hand releases me, I feel life and my tongue surge back into my control.

With all the feelings pent up inside me and the myriad of questions in my mind, I blurt out the most burning of all.

"If you're the prince in charge of this challenge, then what is it?" I demand.

He never turns his head and climbs into the carriage. "Now, now, it wouldn't be fair for me to inform you ahead of the others. You will find out at the same time they will. Isn't this fun?" He clicks his tongue and winks at me.

I wanted to scream at the bastard. A cough comes from over my shoulder. "We will be happy to wait and find out with the others, your Grace." Janice's calm remark angers me.

I turn and verbally pounce on him. "Why did you interject?" I demand.

"There's no point in kicking a dead horse. He's never going to tell you. But it certainly gave him a lot of pleasure to watch you squirm. Why would you give him such entertainment?" Janice crosses his arms while raising both eyebrows.

"He might've told me something," I grumble. I can hear how foolish I sound, but I'm nervous and angry. I want this over with.

"You will never get what you want from Deston. All you're doing is entertaining him, while he terrorizes you. He'll take great delight in it, Sarah. We're playing the long game. When this is all over if you wish, you can seek gratification in torturing him," Janice says, pointing out the obvious.

A smile curls my face at the idea of making Deston dance to my tune, bending him to my will.

Ice fills my veins. *That's what 'they' would do.* That kind of revenge is for the weak, and it's not what I want. No amount of revenge would give me back my life or any of the other lives lost. Toying with the idea makes me no better than them.

I shake my head. "No, you'll never get me that way. Why even suggest that?" I scoff.

Janice counters, "So you can reaffirm it's not who you are. What I saw yesterday, the way you treated Titom, it looked very Fae." Janice crosses his arms.

Our carriage comes to a stop, and I don't reply. I don't wish to discuss it in front of the rest of Deston's Castle. I climb in for the ride.

Breaking the uncomfortable silence, I continue, "Now that we've done the reality check for the morning, what do you think the challenge is?" My eyes trail the landscape outside the window, keeping time with the lurching of the carriage.

"Until we reach our destination," he rambles on.

I interject in surprise, "You don't know where we're going?"

He shakes his head. "I don't. Deston told the drivers, no one else. Until I have more information, I can't possibly provide you with a plan or an idea." His hands clench and unclench.

"Great, you're my trainer and the Minister of war, yet you don't even know where the war's going to be." I wasn't angry at him, just angry at everything. I'm under their control, a piece on a chess board to be moved and maneuvered until the end—check mate.

CHAPTER 6

The ride is short, and as I step out of the carriage I survey the terrain. A large horse arena stands off to the side with a hint of stables around back.

"Deston has brought us to his breeding stables." Janice takes in the surrounding area. His stance is open and ready for an attack.

The footman offers me his hand to help me down from the carriage. Janice leads me to a pen of humans in various staged of transformation. My eyes drift over the other girls. Only two hair colors exist, white and black, but the sea of white in front of me tells me all I needed to know. The chance of a Seelie winning is low. I can understand how easy it is to embrace the fear inside yourself when all you see is death while being inundated with the violence and betrayal.

Hands clap together then begin rubbing back and forth over my shoulder. "Awe, Sarah, you will make me proud today for sure," Deston's voice ebbs over me, cloaking me in a mucky brain fog. I blink to clear my eyes and mind. He continues, "I can show no favorites, my love. But I wish you well." He lifts my hand to his lips, and a thrill zips through my body—along with a gag reflex.

The lie in his words rings in my mind, but my retort gets lost in the malaise, never to reach my lips. Deston drifts away and gains a footing on his floating throne. He waves a hand in the direction of a white-haired Fae on a high, floating platform.

A shoulder collides with my back, knocking me off balance. I stumble a few steps then regain my equilibrium. "You can't even keep your feet under you, you'll never make it on a horse. Stupid human." Nikki's voice is nothing more than scraped nails down a blackboard, creating irritation and goosebumps everywhere she goes.

I didn't turn to look at her. I don't want to meet the effeminate features, which are so like Nick's and yet not. Nick's hair had been brown and his eyes hazel-green. Nikki is now green-eyed and white-haired, and baiting is all she's good for.

"Have you gone deaf too?" she demands as her hand shoves me.

I whip around, slamming the side of my hand into her throat. She stumbles back, choking and clawing at her neck.

"Save your strength for what's to come, Nikki. Stop wasting your time on me," I retort.

The hum rises in her chest, along with the hate in her eyes. I allowed the rumble in my chest to create my shield. She releases her magic, only to batter against my protective barrier.

The deep baritone of powerful magic issues a command, cutting our altercation short and delaying the inevitable. "Stand down, fair Nikki, we shall triumph in the long run. Stop toying with the lesser life forms." Jacques' command is enough to pull her back. Apparently, she'd become his pawn or pet, not sure which.

She huffs, turning on a dime, and shoves her way to the front rail.

I spy Jacques from the corner of my eye. His appraising gaze misses nothing. He blows me a kiss and drifts away on his floating platform with his crew.

Deston's herald raises his hands, throwing a silencing wake over the assembled crowd.

"My fellow Fae, we gather once again to witness the challengers, battle against all the Hallowed Hills has to offer. Their ability to push back against the rule of wild is the only path to winning." He pauses to allow the crowd their moment to roar with approval. Then he claps his hands, causing a loud cracking sound to reverberate over the area. "Our challengers have all shown their aptitude to control magic through song. Most have displayed their true colors and allegiances to a court, whether it be Seelie," hissing fills the air only to be drowned out by the singing of what I can only describe as angelic, "or my personal favorite, Unseelie." His chuckle is joined by many. A deep rumbling vibrates the fence posts around us, causing every living thing to tremble.

My eyes seek out Deston. He stands tall on his platform with his arms raised, mouth open wide. The wakes emanating from him are thick with power. His eyes bore into me. The sound rips into my ears and claws down my throat. I can't turn away from him. As the vibrating raises, my ears quake in time with pressure. The noise rattles around inside my head, causing my vision to grow fuzzy at the edges.

Just as quickly as the sound came, it is cut off. The girl standing next to me slumps to the ground. Red blood flows from her ears, and as I crouch down I feel for a pulse. Her head lolls to the side to reveal fixed, staring blue eyes not yet glowing with the inner Fae light. She's dead, not Fae enough to survive the Unseelie call.

"Oh my, I think our little display may have inadvertently killed a challenger," the herald remarks, clapping both hands in front of him and laughing as many in the crowd follow suit. "Back to the matter at hand. There is only one rule. You must ride your horse and command it to return you to this arena. There is no time limit. If I were you, I'd hold on tight, for if you fall it could lead to a terrible fight." The herald gives a close-mouthed giggle. "Choose your ride and choose it well, otherwise it can be hell." He snorts at his own turn of phrase.

I swallow. *Horses. Why does it have to be horses?*

"Horses are easy to control, they only require a firm hand," Janice states.

I blink up at him. "You're kidding, right? The only horse I've ever ridden is Puca. And he's not a horse."

"You survived. He's Fae, so there is no better training to be had in all the realm," Janice remarks.

Searching his face, I can detect no lie or deception. He is in earnest.

"Hold tight to the bridle and keep your body on the horse. That is all you need to do. Every horse eventually returns home to eat or to sleep. They like the comfortable and familiar." Janice's logical response irritates me. It all sounds so easy, but the pessimist in me doubts anything in Fae is ever that easy.

I want something more, but he leads me to a small paddock and the fate that awaits me inside.

CHAPTER 7

The creature gleams a fabulous blinding white in the light. Fae illumination makes everything appear magical and pretty. This is a horse, or at least it looks that way from the back side. In Fae, nothing is what it seems.

What is it with Fae and horses? The Puca transforms teenagers into horses, Puca is a horse sort of, sometimes, now this.

The lacy fur fringes its hooves, and it flicks its tail, causing the hair to flow like a cascading waterfall blown by the wind. Its fur gleams sleek over its hindquarters, exposing the powerful muscles itching to move. It turns its head, revealing a sharp horn protruding from between its eyes.

"It's a fucking unicorn?" I sputter. The laugh I want to release is lodged in my chest as its eyes land on me. My mouth goes slack with fascination.

"It's a Kelpie, and it will kill you. They use their beauty to draw you in. Whatever happens, don't fall off his back or he'll tear you apart, though only in the water. On land, you are perfectly safe." Janice informs me.

My head whips around to meet Janice's pinched face. His hands press a rope into mine.

"It'll eat me? Unicorns are man-eaters? What will you Fae come up with next?" I shake my head and enter the corral.

The wakes moving off the Kelpie are gentle, and they message everywhere they touch. He emanates his own song designed to enchant me. It whispers of love and adventure. Lowering his head, he invites me to climb on to his back for a ride. His eyes lure me to caress him. It is a drugging magic. My will is not my own, and I'm compelled to touch it. My hand stretches out as my heart speeds up— I need to touch the unicorn. He lifts his head and snorts while turning his oily black eyes to me. It sings of happiness unending with him. The stallion stamps his foot in irritation at my reluctance.

"Any contender that does not complete the challenge will be fed to the Pixies," the herald's words ring out and chill me, causing goose bumps to rise. My eyes meet those of a Fae named Rogue. He winks at me. Fae have the uncanny ability to wink one eye without moving any other muscle. The only other creature I know capable of that was a cat.

I bet he's the Original Rogue, the one all else have been named after. Jerk.

It makes my flesh rise and my back itch. The leather bodice and shirt covered the bulges now protruding from my spine. Soon I won't be able to hide my hideously contorted body.

Turning my mind back to the animal in front of me, I sing a sweet song of love. The rope in my hand turns and twists on itself, wrapping around the unicorn's neck. I weave it into a halter. Then, changing the musical magic, I braid the reins in with the stallion's mane.

I cut my magic and leap onto the Kelpie's back. He dances to the side, and his muscles tighten up. The hum from my chest flows around us, along with the braided reins.

I create a magical seat belt. It locks around my waist, weaving itself into my belt, and buckles.

The Kelpie rears, coming down hard on the ground. He screams with irritation at my magical changes. His tail whips around and beats at me. I grip his sides for dear life with my legs. Chomping and grinding come from his mouth as he shakes it from side to side. Then, he turns enough for me to see his eyes roll from the oily black to fire red. He doesn't have whites, but why would he? He's Fae.

Wind pushes at me and stings my cheek, and an itchy, wet feeling inches its way down my neck. I reach to scratch it, only for my hand to come away bloody. Readjusting my seat, I turn— the white tail is tipped a bloody red.

"You fucker, that's my good side too." I swirl my hand in the air, changing the magic wake around us. Then, I open my palm and push it at his tail. The hair tangles into a knot where the spine ends, making it look more like the stump of a pit-bull's tail, rather than that of a regal horse. The stallion screams while leaping into the air and as it takes off at a dead run for the water.

Awe fuck, what the hell had Janice said about Kelpies? I can't recall. The water's edge races to meet us— and it appears to be a stream.

He leaps into the air and the wind whistles past my ears before gravity takes over plunging us both into the watery depths of an ocean like stream.

Blinking away the salty sting, I press my lips together, holding on to as much air as possible.

My fingers whiten with my grip on the bridle. We sink deeper and the pressure on my chest increases.

I won't survive this way. Frantic fear takes over as I thrash, kicking the sides of the kelpie and yanking its mane.

His skin shivers, as does his magic wakes. Then, starting at the nose and flowing back his coat of fur flattens and smooths away into the oily scales, which reveals his fish-like nature.

His tangled mane changes into a dorsal fin. My rope loosens and I begin to float away. Thinking fast, I wrap the loose rope around my left hand. His hindquarters changed into a giant tail moving back and forth. He isn't a unicorn anymore, instead he is part horse, part fish.

The water horse rushes forward, causing the rope to yank my arm and drag me along behind him. My body aligns with his, and every few seconds his strong tail slams into my lower legs.

In a panic, I open my mouth to cry out, and the salty water rushes in to claim the vacant cavern in my chest. Then, I panic, thrashing my arms and legs in a feeble attempt to reach the surface and air.

I'm going to drown. *That's* what Janice said. They make you pass out from lack of air then eat you while you're still alive.

Who would ever think a unicorn was pretty?

In my mind's eye, I see blood dripping from the muzzle and the sharp teeth of a shark filling its mouth. One hoof atop my trampled head with my entrails spread out around my body. *That is never going to happen. Death by unicorn, no fucking way.*

My desire changes the beating of my heart from a thump to a rumble. It vibrates the water around me, lifting the pressure on my lungs. But there is no air down where we are. The ocean knows no end in Fae. I'll fight it till my dying moment, but water is free and flows where it wishes.

Pressure mounts in my skull, pushing in from all sides. Everything takes, on a fuzziness. I can't focus — it's the same as it is around Deston.

Tension in my chest eases, and my cheeks curl at the sides into a stupid grin. The thought of Deston always brings fog. It settles over my mind, slowing my response time. I breathe out warm water that had sat too long in my lungs.

Pain shoots up my left leg, and my eyes clear as my brain screams for more air.

The Kelpie turns, slamming my body into the side of his neck. My face squishes against flaps in the skin. It only has the head of a horse — his neck is covered in gills. They open, releasing warm water, then close. The Kelpie's head moves forward, then pulls back in a rhythmic motion.

The rumble in my own chest changes. Opening my mouth wide, I pull water into the deepest reaches of my lungs. In my mind, I picture a fish and its gills on my neck.

Hot water jets over my shoulders and the pressure in my body equalize. Air… sort of fills my needy lungs and blood. The screaming in my blood vessels eases, drifting away with the warm water flowing through my gills.

The magic changes from a rumble to a purr as my skin hardens. The pressure on my cranium disappears, allowing my ears to release the trapped air. Sighing in relief, I have reached parity with the sea.

With narrowed eyes, I spy Aqualis the water nymph following us.

"I suppose you're here to take over the seas? I say no." Aqualis spats, then slithering up and down with the movements of her liquid body, pushing to keep up with the Kelpie.

"I don't want to take over, you silly fish, I just want to survive," I retort.

She narrows her eyes, allowing a smile to spread, revealing rows of long sharp teeth. "Only the strong survive Fae." She replies, then stretches out her hand— it carries a dagger. In one motion, the rope is severed.

The ache in my shoulder eases and I float away as the Kelpie continues on his way. The rope around my wrist untwines revealing the chewed skin where the rope had eaten into my flesh.

Aqualis instructs, "Eat, Zephyr my pretty. She will be a tasty prize."

All the while she trails a finger from the Kelpie's nose up between its ears. Its oily black eyes instantly turn red, and it dives for me.

All those hours running and fighting with Janice weren't wasted. My muscles tighten, ready to spring. Zephyr's head lowers the closer he comes, angling the horn at me. I hum webbing into my hands and feet.

My rope halter hangs loosely around his neck. Underwater breathing has equalized my buoyancy, so I didn't sink or rise, only linger in one spot. The motion of the water itself moves me. If I time it right…

Zephyr's momentum pushes a large volume of water at me, and I kick to the side just as he reaches me. He turns his head, allowing razor-sharp side fins to slice into the flesh of my tricep; salt pours in while blood and cries pour out.

I missed my chance, and I watch as the end of the rope pulls away, along with Zephyr's tail.

Aqualis taunts, "He won't miss again, little human. You may have Fae in your blood but you will never be one of us." Her laugh ripples through the water. An orange, cloudy haze lingers in the water surrounding me.

Ripping what was left of my sleeve off, I wrap it around my arm to stem the tide of blood, but the taste is already out there, and it floats in the water around us. Even my vision is clouded with it. The haze of diluted blood swirls around me with every move, like food coloring at an Easter-egg-dyeing party.

"Zephyr, so smart of you to call the others." Aqualis voice is warm as liquid honey, and just as sticky and sweet.

"More? He called more with my blood?" I demand, hoping to hide my fear.

In the distance, I spy a wall of sea-green shadows. Mustering my strength, I dive for whatever it is. Slowly, the outline of a kelp forest looms in front of me. I can hide, but it can't hide the sweet scent of blood trailing behind me in the water. I had to staunch the bleeding.

Water flows over my gills, but it's barely a degree warmer than when it enters my chest due to my frantic breathing. Darting my eyes up and down, I'm as agitated as any animal who's being chased by a superior predator. I can swim all I like, but with my wounds, they will follow me as surely as Hansel and Gretel followed the rocky trail home.

Not everything is what you think, though, black is white and white is black. Maybe up is down. I dive down, kicking my legs for all the power I can squeeze out of them and pull a dagger from my bodice.

This better work. The rumble in my chest rises, moving out from my body and into the shiny metallic blade. The silver glows pink, then bright golden orange.

Pulling the wrap from my arm with shaking hands and white knuckles, *I can do this,* I press the blade to the gash in my arm and scream. The water pressure in my ears rises, pressing into my skull. As I pull the dagger back, tremor's rack my body. I survey the wound — I'd only cauterized part of it.

Damn it, I shouldn't have closed my eyes. Biting my lip, I let the rumble rise again.

A click and a snort is all the warning I get before the pressure of the water pushes me back and a horn punctures my side.

Aqualis giggles. "Yes, kill her now! Get it over with." The bubbling laugh of treacherous water fills my ears.

My blade floats up over my head as my vision fogs with pain and blood. The sea horse continues pushing my impaled body through the water.

The rumble in my chest is still there, holding the unreleased magic. Locking my eyes on the unicorn's horn, I set the magic free.

The sickening sound of bone snapping frees me from the Kelpie. It screams and turns to bite me. Using the force from the water, I allow it to push my body out of range.

Water enters the deep recesses of my lungs the rumble rises again. Pain radiates from my arm and impaled side. I can't swim away fast enough to survive this.

The Kelpie with the broken horn moves away, then turns for the next charge.

Magic moves around me like a mist, bending to my will and rushing out to the kelp forest. It comes alive, wrapping around Aqualis and the Kelpie at the same time. The ocean forest works itself over into a tangled jail.

Aqualis screeches in frustration. "This won't hold me. I'll be out before you can get away, and then I'll free Ansta. She will feed you alive to her colts for taking her horn." Aqualis taunts me with her vision of being eaten alive. I need to get out of here. Whipping my head around, I spy Zephyr charging me from a different direction.

Desperate to get away, I swim to Ansta's trapped form and climb on her back. Her tail lashes as her body squirms around desperate to unseat me, but the kelp ropes hold her firm.

Ansta cries and snorts, causing Zephyr to pull up short, ceasing his forward motion. I twine the rope-like kelp around my good arm. The wakes in the water are a mess. I can't make out who they are coming from. They're large and pained.

Aqualis calls out, "She's weak, Zephyr, kill her now!" Aqualis aura wakes with fear and rage.

I pant to control my pain, laboring over every breath. The rainbow crystals of the horn protruding from my side aches and my blood clings to the scales on Ansta's back.

Ansta's head droops, with the loss of her horn, her color fading with every passing moment. I, too, feel the weakening of my body. The bleeding from my arm increases with every flex.

Leaning over, I press my face to one side of her neck. "I'll give you your horn back, Ansta, and heal you if you take me to the surface." Biting my lip and holding my liquid breath, I wait. She shakes her skin, letting it ripple from her mouth to tail. The wave of the ripple crests with her change from sea to land, scale to fur, fish to unicorn.

I pull out another dagger and cut us free from the kelp forest. A hum rattles in my throat, weaving the kelp around me and into the Kelpie's mane. I hold tight to the dagger out of sheer fear.

As water pushes at me, trying to force me from the Kelpie's back, blackness edges my vision. My muscles push at the horn in my side, causing pain to course over my belly and race down into every cell.

Stay awake.

CHAPTER 8

We push through the surface of the water like a finger through a balloon, and I choke as my nose meets the scent of wet horse and soil, but I can't suck in air. My body presses in heavy on me, pressure works both ways. I hum, but no sound comes forth. I changed my body for the water pressure, and now it's crushing me.

The rumbling in my chest rises but is only enough to change my lungs not the rest. I remain heavy, and the weight crushes the air from my lungs, forcing it to leak out.

I lost my dagger when I passed through the surface of the water and I am left to unwind the kelp from my good arm, allowing it to fall away. Ansta neighs and tosses her head. But her color is dingey, all her gloss and glow gone with her horn. No magic wakes from her form.

I grope for my pouch and the energy vial Lavender left there. My fingers dig into the dark bag, landing on the tiny bottle, then bring it to my other hand. My arm muscles don't want to cooperate, they strain against the pressure of land. My fingers won't grip the bottle, so I wedge the tiny vial between my thumb and index finger, then squeeze. Pain tears up my arm into the tendons and muscles at my wrists and elbows. Panting, I twist the lid off with my other hand, but at the last second my grip slips, tipping the contents into my lap. I watch in horror as it cascades out.

The energy in the vail drains away, along with my strength. Searching the inside of the lid, I find a light film of moisture there, it could be enough. Licking the inside of the lid, I receive a split-second rush, but it fades far too quickly.

One drop remains on my bad hand. Using my other hand, I lift it to my mouth and suck the remaining potion off. It tastes diluted by ocean water. Power rushes through my veins, but it wouldn't last, I have to work quickly.

My fingers rip at the kelp, tearing it away and freeing my body. Bending my left knee, I shift my weight to the side with the horn protruding. My foot never makes it over the Kelpie's spine. I slide to the ground, landing hard on my injured side, and a scream escapes. Ansta shakes her coat, forcing the kelp to fall away.

Digging my fingers into the soil around me, I push to stand up. Pain shoots through my flexing muscles. The movement around the horn loosens it, and blood oozes around its edges.

Panting, I implore Ansta, "Turn your head to me and crouch down, I can't stand up."

The oily black eye surveys my wound. She sniffs at my hands and belly. The Kelpie bends her knees and lowers her chest to the ground, followed by her hindquarters. She blinks at me, snorting and tossing her head while nudging my shoulder. The beating of my heart speeds up as my breathing grows ragged. *I have to do this.*

"Are you going to keep your word?" Aqualis demands in her watery voice, which pours over me like a raging river ready to burst its banks.

Panting, I reply, "Yes, if I can." My breathing is shallow and labored. Tingles fire at my side, numbing me from the waist down.

She rushes on, "You gave your word. In Fae, you can't go back. You can't lie, or welsh once a deal is struck." Aqualis' voice has a pleading undertone. She *needs* me to keep my word.

I slowly remark, "I don't lie. Fae do." Then, I heave a sigh and move my left hand to the site of the wound. With quick panting breaths, I wrap my good hand around the horn. Then, squeezing my eyes shut, I pull. The rough edges of the horn scrape the meat as it exits my flesh followed by a sucking pop.

A roar rakes over my raw throat. My eyes open to blood pouring from the hole in my side. Tears stream down my cheeks and I shudder. Then, I tentatively press my left hand over the gaping hole. I can't stop the bleeding, not the way my left arm is since I am unable to create pressure.

The Kelpie lowers her head to my lap, and I turn the horn over in my hand. Wakes from the Kelpie's head and the horn reach out to one another. Aligning my broken end with the stump between her eyes, I fit it back together with a click. The magic around her is desperate to be mended. I let the rumble in my chest begin. The larger the magic's pull, the heavier my eyes grow. I can barely fight to keep them open. The sweet sound of an opera invades my mind and my magic. Something from The Magic Flute fills the air around us, then crashes. My hand falls away from the Kelpie's head, but the horn stays.

A smile touches my lips and I release a sigh. The sound of fur shaking drifts at the edge of my awareness. I let it slip away as I slide back onto the grass. The cavern roof is covered in the day-glo colors of a mosaicked Fae sky—I can finally see it. I wonder if the Fae painted it that way to remind them of the surface after they were forced down here?

My chest rises and falls, air entering and leaving through my nose. The pressure around my head is tight, like one of the nine circles of hell. When I turn my head, the bumps that encircle it acting like the notches on a gear. My torso presses back on my spine and the hunch growing there.

None of that matters, not the pain or loss. My heart pumps the blood from my body at a rapid pace, I can't heal it. Nick and Arty aren't here to help or save me. My eyes burn with unshed tears, and I try to swallow them, but they won't go down, instead sticking in my throat, and choking me. Rubbing my hot eyelids does nothing more than spread blood over my face. The fingers pressing at my wound grow slippery with viscous fluid pouring out. Pain pounds with my heart, every beat leaking my life away.

Aqualis cuts into my pained haze. "Don't die, my Lady! You must live, for we have great need of a Fae such as you." The watery voice dripped with a promise of refreshment. Her hand bathes my face, covering it warm water, smoothing moisture across my lips.

"I swear fealty to you and only you. All the power of water is at your disposal. Use it as you may." Aqualis's whispered words meet my ears, but do not soak in.

A warmth spreads to every cell and I float away with it, riding it. If death is a wave, I want it to be just like this. The warm embrace of its deadly wet kiss soothes me, raising me up with a swell and bringing me down in a trough. I rock on this ocean of death. The surf carries me on my ride, bubbling and frothing around me.

"Sarah." Vibrations so familiar meet me on my death wave.

I sigh, it's easier now. "I'm swimming away," I reply, allowing my words to drift to no one in particular. A fiery pain covers the left then right side of my face.

"Sarah, wake up!" Janice's words filter through the watery surge. I love the sound of his voice, so deep and rich. I picture his lips, defined and full as he says my name. My only desire is to listen to his voice forever.

"Sarah! Stay with us, Sarah!" His voice colors my warm wave with desperation and fear. *Why is everyone so afraid of death?* The fire meets either side of my face once again. Eyes shoot open, then narrow, bringing an opening for the pounding in my chest to return.

"Lavender, give me another vial. I can't heal her this close to death." Janice's brows scrunch together, creasing his smooth skin with worry. I want to touch his beautiful face, but my hand wouldn't move. The beautiful wave of death recedes as desire pushes it back—my desire.

"Open your mouth, Sarah. Drink this!" Janice demands. His violet eyes are pinched and pleading with me.

My lips part for the liquid fire to drip down my throat. The first vial forces my eyes open wide. I choke on the second, and the third jolts my body up into a sitting position.

"Sing with me, Sarah, and I'll close the wound." Janice orders. Electric lightning runs through my veins. My vision fills with the giant purple mushrooms surrounding my body, like crumbs following me in a trail from the Kelpie to my present position.

"Sarah, focus on me!" Janice hand cups my burned cheek. He turns my face, forcing me to meet his violet eyes. I blink, to clear my vision.

"Janice, I...I had to save her. She was dying." My explanation comes out weak and squeaky.

"Yes of course you did. Now I need to save you." His lips part into a smile as he sings. Musical magic wakes wave over me, tickling my side and arm. The tickle becomes an itch then, a scorching burn. The sound of his voice fills my ears and cauterizes my wounds. Trembling with the vibrations of his magic, it tears at my muscles and tendons. Demanding my body to heal. My throat turns to raw meat with my screams. Every cell is lit on fire, and my belly roars with hunger. My face tingles and shivers when the magic abruptly ceases.

Pushing the hair back from my forehead, he lays a kiss on my brow on the scarred side. "I'm sorry I can't heal anymore." He turns to Lavender. "Quick, clean her up, make it look like a scrape and nothing more." Janice is up and in two steps next to the Kelpie.

Ansta bows her head to him, and he runs his hand from her cheek down her neck. She touches him ever so gently with the tip of her horn and it glistens with a liquid.

"Thank you, sweet Ansta. Wait for the audience to pass on your gift. It will further our bid." She tosses her head and snorts while pawing the ground.

"Sit up, my lady, quickly. We can't let the others know you've been healed by anyone." Lavender drags me up, clasping my injured wrist, forcing me to cry out. Searching my body, I find the gash in my side, and the skin is folded back allowing me to see the red, meaty flesh inside. It still oozes blood, but it's more of a superficial wound than the gaping hole it had been.

My left arm aches from the tear in my shoulder muscle. Janice healed me just enough to live, but that's it.

"Aqualis, get rid of the giant mushrooms or they'll know we healed her," Janice orders.

Aqualis sings of trees falling in a forest, and one by one they all fall in the water to be dragged away by Kelpie's, leaving behind only the small dribbled trail of mushrooms.

The energy rush from the vials lingers, but I'll burn through that in no time.

"Did I pass?" I inquire absently. Why that even matters I don't know.

Janice responds with a smile, "Yes, you passed. Others did too, which is why we have this chance to help you." His eyes say something, but I can't follow.

My mind muddles with pain and hunger. "Why am I so hungry?" I demand, rubbing my hand across my belly careful to miss my wound.

Janice instantly responds, "Because you've been gone for three days. Did Ansta save you?" Janice's wavers with his query.

"No, she stabbed me with her horn, and I broke it off. I promised to put it back if she took me back to the surface," I absently supply.

He kicked at the kelp lying on the ground. "You were in the kelp fields?" he scoffs. "Kelpie hide their young there. You must have been too close to her colts, so she attacked." He scratches at his hairless chin.

"Whatever her reason, that crazy water nymph over there rooted them on." I wave my hand at Aqualis.

Lavender sniffs at Aqualis, then turns her back on Aqualis. I just want to get away from the wet bitch.

"I'm sorry, my lady," Aqualis spouts, sporting a petulant pout.

"Don't *my lady*, me, you crazy bitch. First, you burn half my face off, then you tell the crazy unicorns to kill me and feed me to their young. Fuck you!" I reply, the fear of death sharpening my mind back from my deathly malaise. I didn't get to say more; slashing water came from the river.

There seated on a Kelpie stallion is Nikki. Her white hair is plastered down her back, and a giant smile on her face. She is untouched and regal as if she hadn't a single worry. A smirk hitches her face and she remarks, "Oh, Sarah, are you hurt? Did your Kelpie buck you off and have a snack?" All the while, she pretends to hide her giggle behind the back of her hand.

I retort, "I finished, though I'm not sure everyone else did. It isn't a laughing matter, Nikki. Don't you feel anything for all those girls that died? Or is this all about Nikki looking clever?" I want to stand up and face her, but my strength isn't there.

She never takes the smile from her face. She raises both eyebrows then slowly lowers them while narrowing her eyes then shifting from left to right. "I didn't kill them, so why should I feel bad or good or anything? I didn't even know them, these girls you say have died. Why should I care? When you're done wallowing in the mud, maybe you can see it from my point of view. Peasants don't matter." She clicks her tongue and heels her seahorse in the belly. They both trot away.

The ground around me is trampled and muddy. "Help me up please. Get me back to the arena," I request.

Nikki's words disturb me. How can she not care what happens to any of the other contenders? *She'd called them peasants, like a Fae.*

Janice grasps me under my arms and pulls me into a standing position. We still aren't eye to eye, but I had perfect alignment with his lips, and the full sensual pout they form. I force myself to meet his eyes. They bore into me, shifting from my lips to my eyes and back again.

His aura becomes a fiery flame. He hasn't removed his hand from under my arms. I don't want him to. Instead I want, him to lean in and…

"My lord, my lady, they come," Lavender's words break the spell.

Janice steps away and turns his back to me. The fire in his aura quickly dissipates with Deston's arrival.

CHAPTER 9

I tear my eyes away from Janice's fading aura.

Deston's smile carries no hint of worry or concern. Instantly, my mind is slammed with a foggy malaise. I mentally claw at the edges, but in my weakened state, it is nothing more than fingers digging into a muddy cliff unable to find purchase.

"My dearest Sarah, you survived. I feared the worst on the second day. But here you are with barely a scratch." His words send an electric thrill through me, causing me to forget the gash in my side and the torn flesh of my wrist. Instead, I bathe in his attention, soaking it up.

"We should get you back to the arena so all Fae may share the joy I feel at your survival." His proclamation was enough for me. He extends his arm in front of me. My body wants to place my hand over it, but my mind screams no.

Janice leans in and murmurs to Deston, "Your Grace, the Kelpie wishes to extend a gift."

My weakness returns with a vengeance and my knees shake to keep me upright. Ansta paces to my side, nodding her head, and snorts. Without a by your leave, I find myself seated on her back. She snorts again and moves away from the group. The fog drifts away with every step, like pulling back a curtain.

"The Kelpie has a mind all of her own." Deston's dry laugh follows me.

Aqualis splashes into the conversation. "Ansta is simply seeking to ingratiate herself, as are we all." Aqualis' watery lie speaks volumes—she is covering for the unicorn. I lean into Ansta's mane humming the hair into reins, her body cradles mine.

The roar of a crowd off in the distance alerts me to my fleeting respite.

Lavender informs me, "My Lady, you must gather your strength for the mob, as you must appear strong and triumphant." Lavender sings changes to my hair and makeup. I don't know why, as no amount of magic would remove the ugly scar covering half my face.

My shirt is torn from the shoulder, I have a big rip in my bodice, there's blue-ish red blood all over my lower body, and half my face looks like fairy Barbie sat too close to a blow torch.

"Lavender, stop primping me, I am a waste of your great talent. I will never be a perfect, pretty Fae." My curt words cut her ministrations short.

.

Deston remarks, "No, your scars make you more Fae than you know. I see the beauty within, not without. Allow Lavender her little touches. It is all she's good for." Deston's proximity brings the fog on anew.

Lavender stills, pressing her lips together and working them back and forth.

I bristle at his cruelty. Lavender is not a good-for-nothing. But I can't wipe away the fog long enough to dig up a retort, and the stupid smile on my face does nothing to reveal my true feelings. Lavender visibly sinks in on herself.

Deston places his hand on my thigh. "Allow me the honor of holding your hand." It wasn't a question, but an order. My hand moves of its own accord. I'm his automaton, a puppet.

The touch energizes my skin, but it doesn't reach the rest of me, only skims the surface.

I am bone tired, and the energy closes in like a net covering me. The fog races over me and becomes a wall my mind can't break through.

I see the crowd and hear the cheering, but it never touches me. Nikki stands in front like a conquering hero. She kicks her Kelpie in the side and whistles, forcing the unicorn to bow before the crowd. The crowd screams with wild abandon in response.

"Wild is here," Aqualis whispers the words, and her voice quakes with fear and trepidation. Ansta shivers, shaking her head from side to side. Lavender's hair pales.

Deston's grip on my hand tightens. "Wild is good, we should welcome the wild," Deston replies, laughing. It doesn't make sense to me. The wild of the world is everywhere. *Why did she say that?* I push back on the wall of fog, groping for enough clarity and understanding to grasp their words. Mimicking Ansta, I shiver and shake my head. The Kelpie snorts in approval.

Words whisper through my mental malaise, "Fight, my lady, you must fight Fae to win it." Ansta's thoughts reach me but slide away like water over an oily surface. The heaving in the unicorns' muscles causes her chest to quake.

"The Resister survives." The voice of a strange Fae lifts above the others to announce my arrival.

Nikki kicks her horse to block my forward motion.

"I'm the winner here, you are nothing. You barely survived." Her retort wakes her anger into my foggy world. I can't muster the strength to reply. Ansta rears at the other unicorn, Deston releases my hand, taking several steps away from the dangerous confrontation. The two Kelpie skirt each other.

"You can't even control your horse. Pathetic." Nikki sneers at me. The fog pulls back, and my mind sharpens like a blade to a whetstone.

I reply, "Control is an illusion as is most of Fae. I thought you would have learned that by now. Ansta is asking your stallion to move. You had your moment in the light, now it's mine." I bare my teeth to her. I don't want a moment in the light, but Fae only respect power, and I know I must show some. I pat Ansta's neck, and she releases a scream at the male water horse and raises a leg as if to kick him. The other Kelpie dances out of our way. Nikki kicks him repeatedly in the belly, to no avail. Ansta snorts and neighs at him. He bows his head and backs away.

Nikki huffs, "Get in front of them, you worthless beast." The Kelpie kicks his hindquarters in response to her forceful magic. She tilts to the side and whistles at him again. Ansta moves into the winner's circle. I whip my head around in time to witness the water horse buck, with Nikki screaming at him. Nikki rumbles her magic in her chest before freeing it to wake over the stallion attacking the poor Kelpie. He responds by lying down on the muddy ground with the force of her abuse.

I, in turn, pat Ansta's neck and she tosses her head.

The rest of Fae screams and cheers. Some are calling my name, others hissing. Deston's herald rouses the crowd with all nature of rhyming. Deston takes back his seat on the floating throne and drifts away on my adulation. The cornucopia of noise buffets my sides. I raise my hand to push back on the battering wakes, only to find silence and wide staring eyes.

"You wish to regale us with your challenge?" The herald's tentative question catches me off guard.

I am taken aback at the obedience of the crowd. "No, I simply wish for quiet and a meal," I answer.

Janice offers his hand, which I promptly take, kicking my legs over the side and sliding off the unicorns' back.

My legs threaten to buckle under me, but a force of magic from the water horse keeps me upright. I pat Ansta's neck, the only way to thank her without words.

Her oily black eye bats a lash at me as she speaks, "I wish to impart a gift to you, one only I can give." Ansta's hindquarters dance to the side, allowing her to turn and face me full on. The arena quiets with the unicorn's words.

"Take my gift and be whole." There at the tip of her crystalline horn glistens a drop of liquid. Ansta tilts her head down, angling it to my mouth.

Janice voices the answer I'd been wondering, saying, "It's a healing potion, only a unicorn can heal all that ails you, including your scars."

I open my mouth to receive the drop, but a gust of air pushes it off course and it lands on my scarred cheek, spreading a burning sensation over the area. I rub my finger across the pained region, but it's dry and soft as baby skin. I refocus on the world around me. The breeze waked from Deston. My eyes narrow at him. His eyes widen with false shock, but his aura colors with the deceit of his actions. Deep in the heart of Deston lies the black rot of hate. He despises and envies me.

I grind my teeth and stretch a smile over my face. The pull from my scar is less than before. Fae may love beauty, but they love a good fight better.

A black-haired Fae leaned over the side of bleachers. "She carries the blue blood of Tuatha Dé Danan," he screams the announcement with wild abandon. The crowd roars and shrieks, clawing at one another. They began to clamor over the sides of the protective rail.

My Unicorn rears back, kicking at the oncoming masses. Ansta orders, "Take her before the wild does." A vise grip takes ahold of my arm, dragging me away from the Unicorn and the mindless horde.

Janice pulls me along with him and thrust me into the carriage, slamming the door in my face. The body of the carriage shifts with the weight of someone jumping on it. I fall back into the seat with the force of our forward motion. A whip cracks the air ahead of us. I tumble from one side to the other.

The ache in my side rears its head again, and I instinctively covered my wound with my hand, only to find blood flowing freely again. The shifting in the carriage thrusts me into the seat. The last thing I remember is my face closing in on the door frame before impact.

CHAPTER 10

I raise my sword above my head with two hands, then bring it down to waist level and stop. Then, I parry with a diagonal slash from right to left, going over the fighting motions my sword master taught me. Practice makes perfect and will keep me alive. I have to ignore the ache in my side and the almost healed wound in my thigh. They do nothing but remind me I'm nothing more than a Fae pin cushion.

Janice breaks in, "You're getting better, but you need to move faster. Keep your guard up at all times. Also, you're not using your pommel or quillons enough. Remember, dead is still dead, whether you stab them in the heart with the blade or eye with a quillon. You can kill someone by bludgeoning them in the head with the pommel of your sword." Janice raises his sword.

"Right, let's go again." Readying my sword in a defensive position, I lunge forward. Janice dances out of the way with a twirl and the grace of a ballet dancer. If didn't know better, I'd think he was *Baryshnikov*. Only taller with short black hair.

I missed, so I retreat, doing my own version of a pirouette, then a fade back to the right. After a short advance forward, I position my feet in an open stance, presenting the true edge of my blade, and slash down. Janice barely makes it out of range. The front of his shirt falls open to reveal a scratched trail of blue blood.

"Very good, you drew blood. Excellent! You're getting better. A few more enchantments on your armor and weapons and I think we might have you somewhere you can win." His lips curve up slightly at the edges in an approving smile.

The one I'm always looking for. I don't know why I want it, but I do.

"Why exactly do I need to learn to swordfight and be good enough to beat you?" I lower my sword and step back, allowing my shoulders to relax. I touch the tip of the blade down into the ground, then rest my hand lightly on it as if it was a cane.

"Everything I teach you is so you can win," he quickly responds.

"They will push for the final challenge, so you need to be ready." He whips his sword around in his hand. I watch as it swirls in a circle.

The pommel whirls in a circle in his hand before he clasps the hilt again.

"Great, I don't feel ready. All those girls… what happens to the ones that survived but weren't good enough?" I cross one leg in front of the other, putting the tip of my toe on the ground and one hand on my hip.

Janice tips his head back and heaves a sigh. "You know as well as I do, they died—thousands, perhaps. The only way to end it is if you win. You've seen some of your competition; if they win, death will float across the planet led by an army, decimating humanity and anything else. I don't know why I have to keep repeating this to you. I know you understand, and yet you rail against the problem and the process. I know it's not fair, but life is not fair, Sarah. If life was fair our queen would still be alive and you would be on the surface playing games with your friends. Instead, you're down here killing everything that you can and learning to kill more."

Janice steps forward.

"Keep practicing your sword positions, and your footwork." He turns and walks away.

I thought I improved, so maybe I was getting better. *I am never going to beat him. He's the minister of Joust and War, for God sakes. He's probably been studying swordplay for 1000 years.*

Snickering in the background draws my attention away from my inner musings. Two Fae, both with light hair. My eyes narrow, Unseelie. Two sets of almond-shaped eyes laugh at me as their hands cover their mouths, and one leans over to whisper in the other's ear. I can't hear what she said, but I'm sure it was something like 'she sucks' and 'she'll never win'.

Janice said this whole bullshit fight was about nothing more than a crown, and who would lead all these stupid, simpering, self-absorbed, pointy-eared...

Technically I'm pointy eared—well, one pointy ear. Perhaps I should stop calling them bastards?

I take the bait anyway and inquire about their snickering." Something I can help you with?" Sheathing Silver, I put my hand on my hips, letting my fingers dance across the pommel of my sword.

"No, we were just entertained." She waves her hand around, as if somehow I was a performer, simply here for her amusement. I'm not taking that bait. She wants me to ask if she was entertained or how I was doing or something ridiculous like that. As if I actually care what her opinion is.

Biting my lower lip, I release it and slowly respond, "Unless the two of you would like to have a special spell sung just for you, I suggest you back off and stop distracting me." One's eyes widen with fear and the other's narrows with anger.

"I haven't seen you create any new spells. I don't believe you have the ability to create new magic. The only one who can do that is a queen, a true queen, and you're not a queen." She waves her finger at me. Apparently, she isn't afraid I'll cut it off, and I desperately want to.

Truthfully, I can sing some song they haven't heard, bending it to my will. But I'm not going to be baited into her game. She wants to see how powerful I am. I can't lead these people unless they respect me. *Who am I kidding, they are never going to respect me, they'll always see me as the human.* Even if I become queen, my crown will never be safe. Yeah, I may save humanity for a while, but I'll fade, and then who will take my place?

"I think you're right, Lily, I don't think she can create new magic. Only a queen can create new magic," the first Fae remarks.

Wow, minions for fairies and human, are all the same. They just pantomime whatever their crazy leader says.

I can't, I just can't let it go. "I'm sorry, are the both of you laboring under the false delusion I would actually waste my time creating something completely new, just for you?" I look from one set of almond eyes to the other. Lily covers her mouth with the back of her hand again. I'm sure she did it to make herself look cute or adorable, or perhaps she thought it was feminine. I really just find it annoying and the act of a truly shallow mind. It is a calculated move designed specifically to evoke a reaction, my reaction.

I'm out.

Turning my back on them, I grumble under my breath, "Why don't you take a long walk off a short pier?" and move away.

I hadn't taken two steps when Lily's shrill voice cuts the air, "Melody, Melody where are you going? Melody."

I whip my head around to spy Melody's long hair swaying back and forth with the movement of her hips as she glides under the portico, with Lily trailing behind. I don't see why she's so uptight?

Melody doesn't stop till she was halfway across the drawbridge, and then she turns swiftly and leans out over the water. Lily catches her arm at the last moment with one-foot dangling in open air desperately pulling at her. I stop mid-step.

"No, Melody, don't do it." Lily chokes.

"What are you doing?" I demand.

With fear-filled eyes, Lily looks to me. "If she goes in the water she'll die. The fish in there, they eat Fae and human alike. You have to stop her." The unvoiced please lingers in the air.

I rush to Melody's side and grab her other arm, straining with my full body weight to pull her back. "Stop, don't kill yourself, for God's sake," I beg.

The forward pull of her body ceases, and we all slump on the drawbridge in a pile. Melody's eyes stare with a glazed, milky-white entrancement. Her bow-shaped mouth hangs slack. I push back with my feet, sliding over the dirt-covered wood to escape her dead stare.

Lilly's accusing voice follows me. "You did this. How could you do this? Fae can't enchant one another. I don't know who you are, but stay away from us." Lily begins humming.

The wood around me rattles, and the wakes over it change with the new vibrations. Lily's eyes bore into me, her brows pinched down at the bridge of her nose. All around, the hard surface of the wood softens, like a sponge sagging with my weight.

"I didn't enchant her, I didn't do anything." My heart speeds up as Lily's aura changes from purple to black. The air tastes of sinister ash.

"Stop!" Deston's voice booms against the castle wall, bouncing back to pound in my ears.

"You may not attack a challenger. She is under my protection. If you wish to fight, call her for a duel." The chill of his words seeps into my skin as my eyes meet his over Melody's body. *I don't want to duel anyone.*

The wooden surface around me reverts back to normal. Lily lowers her eyes and bites her lip. The hand on Melody's chest curls in as she digs her nails into the skin of her palm. A small drop of blood falls on the bridge and a tiny mushroom sprouts up.

"Sarah, come away from there now." The pull of Deston's voice is more than I can fight off. I obediently stand up, eyes trailing over the amassed crowd to Janice before meeting Deston's face. Something changes inside me, I can't tear my eyes away from Deston, no matter how desperately I want to dart back to Janice's face.

Janice would give me my answers— I trust him. But I could feel the magic forcing me, bending me to its will. It's wrong; I should have free will, and yet I know I don't. Somehow Deston has taken my free will and entranced me. A stupid smile covers on my face and butterflies fill my belly. They're fake—none of it is real.

I demand, "What happened to her? Why did she decide to walk into a withering pond of Fae-eating fish? And who keeps Fae-eating fish around their castle? Honestly, you people." He could control my body, but not my mouth. I'd freed it, but how?

Deston returns my inquiry, "It's not important, Sarah. What is important is you've discovered a new ability, an amazing ability. We shall have to discuss it." He offers his hand, and I automatically reach for and take it. I can hear the calculating in his voice. *We shall have to discuss it?* As if it is his to wield, his new ability? Deston leads me away from the scene. Lily continues whimpering in the background. She is afraid.

I ask, "Can't we do something to help Melody? She's entranced. Nobody should be able to control someone like that." My words sound naive. Even humans control each other, wielding whatever power they can find over each other.

His reply is droll, "Her entrancement or lack thereof is not your concern. It will wear off." He waves his hand in the air dismissively. What a pompous ass.

"Does magic wear off?" My body wants to believe him, but my mind is screaming, run away. I don't think fairy magic wears off. Magic is until it's changed and then it isn't. Releasing a sigh, Deston replies, "Yes, yes, sometimes fairy magic wears off. In her case, it's not relevant one way or another. She's alive in her body, just simply not able to do anything." He never even looks back. Melody is part of his court and he just doesn't give a crap. I throw a glance over my shoulder at Janice following form.

I raise an eyebrow at Janice, but he shakes his head and waves me off. How am I supposed to figure this out if he's not going to help me? I hadn't paid attention to where we were going, my mind so locked on how I am going to help Melody.

What the hell have I done? I finally come to my senses standing in the throne room. "Everyone leave." Deston waves his hand at the courtiers. Male and female alike bow and leave the audience chamber.

CHAPTER 11

Deston takes his seat, flourishing the tails of his jacket as he glides into his throne. Off to the side and on a lower step of the dais sits another chair, a smaller chair. The chair is covered in scrolled flowers and a seat the color of soft velvety buttercup petals.

He waves me over to it, and I automatically approach, though every part of me resists sitting. It is below him. I'm not interested in being anyone's servant. I don't care who they are.

"Sit!" he whispers the command. My body pulls at me to move into the chair. My mind screams a resounding NO. My muscles strain to comply, and I fight to resist. Squeezing my eyes shut, I block out the vision of Deston's smarmy face.

Sweat forms over my lips, and heat rolls down my frame. The trembling of my muscles shakes my sword as my hand's white-knuckle grip holds the haft. I open my eyes and finally see what is causing my malaise, magic wakes working to force my compliance.

Pulling a shaky breath deep into my chest, I began to rumble. pulling the strands of magic this way and that till they disappear or fall to the ground inert.

Releasing the breath I'd held, I allow my form to relax. The strain of fighting the spell lifts, and for the first time since the bubble I can breathe a truly free breath

Now I need answers, but where to begin? With a free breath, I ask. "What did I do to Melody?" It comes out slow and deliberate.

Deston's hands wave the question away. "It doesn't matter. Now sit." A magic wake buffets me passing around my form. I didn't meet his eyes—the spell can't work without eye contact.

I can't back off now, so I continue, "You said we would explore my new ability, so what is it?" I pull air in through my nostrils and push it back out, allowing them to flare.

He sighs. "Charisma. It's rare and powerful along with being fun." His tone tells me everything. He's been using it on me for a while.

It is how he's able to keep me too muddled to speak out. It's also how he was able to kiss me. My stomach churns with everything else he could have done.

In the human world Charisma is just good looks and smooth talking. Here, I can change people's minds by smiling at them or speaking to them. I can control their emotions without touching them, turning them into playthings.

Without missing a beat, I ask, "How does it work?" I hold my head high, but keep my eyes averted.

"It's different for each of us. Some need touch to reinforce their Charisma. Others can use a mere word. As you proved in the courtyard, even a muttered desire can be enough." He laughs. "My brother needs only smile. Or the mention of a name can work the magic." He is telling me he's used them all on me. *Bastard.*

My blood boils with hate. Janice is right, this creature can't be allowed to control or influence a Queen. He's a monster.

"Is there any way to help Melody?" I inquire.

Deston sighs in irritation. "Why does she matter? She's a plaything, nothing more. Go practice on her. Try to remove the magic—it would be interesting to witness." His callous words grate on me.

I want to cut him in half with my blade. I want him to pay for making me kiss him. Saliva fills my mouth, and I have to swallow to keep it all back. The walls hum a warning.

"Titom. Did you use it on him?" I demand.

Deston heaves a sigh. "How boring you are. Of course I did. He hated you. He wanted to 'take you out,' as your kind say. I suggested it might be a good idea." He leans on his elbow, cupping his chin.

I spread my hand, stretching my fingers, then pull them together into a fist. I want to kill him. He knew I would kill Titom if he left me no way out.

Deston brightens. "Why don't you sit? We can discuss all the ways Charisma can be used to your advantage. In the end, it may save your life." I step around the chair, facing the front of the room. I keep my back to Deston, allowing me to survey to the room and at my leisure. Keeping his power over me at bay had become my first priority.

I reply, "I wish to pace out my nervous energy." I mount the steps, examining the walls behind the throne. With slow and measured steps, I keep my eyes away from any possible connection with Deston's.

I hum at the walls and watch the carving change minutely. I could win the walls.

Deston offers, "Charisma is the magic of Queens. A true Queen has the ability to influence all of Fae at its core with Charisma." Deston gives the information away without a purpose.

"You're not a queen, yet you have it. How is that possible?" I inquire. I didn't want him to think I cared about his reply, but I did.

Deston laughs. "I was given this power at birth; my queen blessed me with it as a favor to my mother."

CHAPTER 12

Deston requests again, "Why don't you sit down, Sarah?" He steeples his fingers while his elbows sit on the armrests.

"No," My reply issues before I can think about it. My pulse quickens, and I wrestle with my breathing. *Stay calm, you just started a fight.* "I don't want to." My fingers play over the padded armrest. The silky velvet fabric pushes back at my intrusion. From the corner of my eye, I watch as he arches an eyebrow at me.

He questions my choice. "Does the chair offend you? Should I have them bring a new chair?" Amusement laces his reply.

I'm a toy, a distraction meant to amuse. "No, I don't need a new chair. The chair itself is nothing. It's an object. It's what the chair represents that I find offensive." I breathe deeply through my nose, flaring my nostrils to hide my fear and to keep from biting my lips.

He continues, "What's so offensive about showing a deference in status?"

I gaze around the throne room. He wanted to talk to me, and he wanted me to show I am subservient to him. But he made everyone leave, so he wasn't sure I'd comply. He's afraid. His aura wakes muddy uncertainty.

I ask, "Can you create new magic, Deston?" Change the subject, distract him from his stupid plan.

A dry laugh issues from between his perfect lips. "Magic is not new, nor old, it's your ability to access it. I can access magic." I could hear the lie in his voice. *He's such a liar, I want to stamp my feet.*

I don't know why I expect anything else. After everything I've learned about the UnSeelie court and the mere fact that they're hiding what the hell this competition is all about, I guess I shouldn't expect anything less.

"You're lying, I can hear every falsehood. It reeks from you, resembling rotten meat. Why do you lie to me? You say you're my ally, you say you're here to help me, but when I ask you a question you can't even tell me the truth." I rush ahead, as it's too late to stop now. "I know Fae are natural liars, so you probably can't help yourself. It's truly sad. But you even lie to your own allies." My fingers pick at the flowers on the chair, pulling petals one by one with each lie.

In one motion, Deston pushes off from his throne, leaping up in the air at me. He takes two steps and catches himself. Oops, I hit a raw spot.

The room reverberates before his voice. Wakes of magic move away from his chest to pound everything in its way. I'd never seen Deston use his full strength. The room quakes with his power.

He retorts, "I do not have allies. I have vassals. You are my vassal. You are less than me. You are subservient to me. You are only here to serve me." His words blast in my ears and his aura goes from the genteel red to a bright flaming fire.

I avoid his eyes— that's the key to his power over me. The moment I meet his eyes he will have me do as he wishes. There had to be some kind of key, something that would break it. My eyes dart around the room, looking everywhere but at Deston.

I wasn't afraid, I was angry. The wood withers into its cold, silvery, dying colors. The same cold in my heart. Is he changing the room, or am I?

"At last you reveal yourself. Now I can see who you really are." I wave my finger at him, I still had my sword at my side, but truthfully, there was no way I would ever be able to best him. I wasn't strong enough… yet.

"*Who I really am?* I never lied to you about who I am, Sarah. I told you, I am Lord Deston, one of the four princes. This is my domain." He holds his arms wide and pivots on one foot. It is all theatrics, he thinks he has me and can bend me to his will.

Crossing my arms and keeping my eyes on the floor, I say, "It's all a game, isn't it? All you want me to do is to say 'Yes, I'll be your vassal. Yes, I'm subservient to you, Yes, you're greater than me.' " I cock a hip. "That's not going to happen. The answer is, 'No, I will not sit. No, I will not acknowledge you are greater than me.' " My words boom forth, rattling the windows and walls. *Two can play at loud and powerful.* "You wish to strike me down? Go for it. You will never rule through me. I don't care what you say or what kind of spell you put on me. And I know you've put a spell on me. I will not sit in that chair. I will not abdicate to you, a lesser Fae." My nose curls up on one side. "You said so yourself, you're a prince— one of four— you're not even unusual or special. There's four of you, so no I don't want to sit in your chair or play this game anymore, Deston." I uncross my arms. "If you have another candidate in the wings that you think can win, I suggest you bring her on and put me out to pasture. I'm not fighting for you." I paste a half smile over my scarred face and wait.

The waking of the room freezes in place, and even the air ceases to move. He is in front of me in an instant, his forehead pressing down on mine. The heat from his eyes bore into me. I keep my gaze firmly planted on the floor. His contact usually creates a fluttering in my belly, but it didn't affect me in the least this time.

"You liked it when I kissed you." He gives a low, seductive laugh. "I saw the magic flowing from you, you wanted more," he whispers, pressing his mouth to my good ear.

I tilt my head back and huff. "You really are thick. If the world was flooded with piss and you owned the only tree, I wouldn't climb up in it with you. I'd rather wallow in a bath of warm piss for all time than be near you again." His eyelashes tickle my cheek as he blinks at me, determined to ensnare me again with Charisma. Then, releasing a warm breath, he returns to his chair and reclines, lifting the back of his hand to his lips and allowing a half smile of amusement to play across them. Deston sighs. "You may change your mind in time."

Wow, I hate arrogant guys. "I will never sit beneath you, let's get that clear."

He waves his hand away as if my words mean nothing to him.

What an asshole. My eyes trail around the room, landing on a small platform behind Deston's throne, just big enough to set a chair on. I snatch up my chair and set it on the platform, then plop down before he can say a word.

"I will never be your equal and I will never be beneath you. Are we clear, Deston?" I sit straight as a board, arms to either side, eyes staring out the arched entry.

He leaps up, stepping around his own throne, then leans down puts his face directly in my line of sight with both hands on either armrest. His breath on my face and his eyes searching to meet mine, as I dart this way and that. It is the chase of a predator and prey. Eyes glancing at his lips, sides of the room, down at his hands, sliding every which way.

"Look at me, Sarah," he demands.

I lock my eyes onto his ridiculous little shoes. They actually came to a point with a little curl at the end. They were green and soft, like something an elf would wear from a fairytale story.

I calmly reply, "No, Deston I don't think I will. I like where I'm sitting right now. I like being in control of myself. I have a feeling I'm only gonna get stronger, so your little farce will only work for a little while. Just like your rule here, your reign, whatever you call it, eventually it too will have to answer to a higher power—me." The muscles in my face work as I smirk. I let my eyes narrow and dart from side to side. The aching around my head grows. I want to reach up and scratch the ring of bumps forming there. But I can't flinch. Instead, I take my hands and steeple them across my body, allowing my fingers to tap each other, and I wait.

He backs off, huffing irritation, followed by feet slamming against the parquet floor as he charges through the back archway.

I lift my eyes from the floor, taking in the room. It is in full bloom and heavy with a flowery scent; his castle is happy.

Well, I think I won that battle.

CHAPTER 13

"You should not have goaded him." Janice's voice reverberates around the room, sucking all the happiness I had right out of me.

"Are you here to give me strategy shit now? 'How I should play my hand better and Deston is a formidable enemy, and how I should watch my back?' " I lean back on my makeshift throne, letting the tips of my fingers play across my lips.

"You've revealed yourself to him, by Danu. Why didn't you just take out a sign that said I am your enemy and you must try and kill me?" Janice scratches the back of his neck, then and begins pacing the room.

"So, is he lying to me about Charisma?" I demand. The guilt of Melody's behavior still weighs on me. I told her to jump to her death just because I didn't like her.

"What he told you is true Charisma is extremely dangerous and those who have the ability to wield it render the weak helpless. Only the strong-willed can resist its magnetic pull. Why didn't you tell me there was something going on between you and Deston?"

His look of concern is touching… or is it jealousy? Sitting forward, I lean my elbows on my kneecaps and let my head hang down for a minute before I look up at him.

"I don't know, I was conflicted. I… when I looked at him I felt stuff I didn't understand." I held my hands up, shrugging my shoulders.

"You felt conflicted about what?" he demands.

Everything in my chest clenches. What am I supposed to say? *Every time I look at you I feel the same thing as when I looked at Deston?* I can't say that. "You know, I'm just confused. Is a girl not allowed to be confused?" I retort.

Janice turns to survey the room. "This is not a good place to have this discussion. Let us go elsewhere." He turns on a heel to leave.

I don't want to leave the room, I'm comfortable sitting where I am. As a matter of fact, my view isn't as good as it should be. Standing up, I grab my chair and kick the podium in front of Deston's 'throne,' and then plop back down.

"Sarah, you're playing a very dangerous game. We need to leave."

I wave my hand and give a whistle, causing all the windows and doors to seal themselves shut.

"I think we can speak freely now. What do you think?"

His slow, deliberate movements should have been my warning, but I'm not paying attention. I am having fun and it feels good.

Janice slowly enunciates every word, saying, "You cannot flaunt your power in Deston's castle this way. I don't care what you think you've won. You haven't won yet, and right now all you're doing is flirting with further disaster. Open the doors, we need to leave." He waits at the main entrance, his back to me.

I stand up and release a sigh. "Fine I'll leave, though I don't care if I pissed him off," I reply, blowing my bangs out of my face.

"You wish to rule these people, Sarah? You cannot rule through stupidity. What you're doing right now is shortsighted.

This is Deston's domain. No matter what control you think you have over this room, you do not control his domain. This land agreed to be part of his territory long before you were ever born, thought of, or even a glimmer in your father's eye. This room likes you, that's it. You don't own the castle and you don't own the soil—it hasn't given you allegiance. It belongs to Deston. Deston rules, and the only way you can demand anything from it is either win it over or take it. Do you understand what that means?" he inquires calmly.

Yeah, I understand what he meant. If I want to rule, I have to win. If I want to rule just this little square, I have to kill Deston. Like a petulant child, I stand up and huff for a minute, remove the chair from the pedestal, then set it back down on the step and leave. Defying someone in private is one thing, I shouldn't publicly humiliate them. I should have learned that lesson with Titom, but I didn't. I have already made it clear I'm his enemy. I don't have to embarrass him in front of all of his subjects.

"You must release the doors. You're already stronger than I am, and I cannot make you," Janice quietly remarks.

My eyes widen in shock as my mouth opens and closes a few times like a guppy fish. Waving my hand opens the doors, then I return the room to its previous state.

"Can we go practice fighting somewhere else? I don't know if I can handle another moment inside a castle that belongs to someone else." I mumble.

Janice gives me a sharp nod. "Follow me!" Then, he leads me out of the castle proper into the courtyard and under the portico. We crossed the drawbridge and out into a greenfield. Where I take a deep breath, the smell of millions of different types of perfume waft through the air, like little pockets of deliciousness. If you're down near the ocean's edge you might get a whiff of marshland or the tangy salt of the sea. And if you're walking along a meadow, you may come across the scent of daisies or clovers. They won't even have to be anywhere around you—simply a little fog of scent that surrounds you and then quickly lets you go.

I drink it in, opening my mouth and letting the scents engulf my taste buds then blowing the flavored scent out through my nose. Flowers bloom everywhere, big blood-red poppies with their jet-black centers and large, lazy petals.

"Why is it the flowers here just seem so much bigger and brighter? On the surface, you have to put the flower right up to your nose to get a whiff, but here it's everywhere. It's floating around like little bubbles of floral happiness."

Janice replies, "The surface flowers are a shadowy copy of their brothers and sisters here in the Hallowed Hills. It's the Fae lighting, magic fairy light woos every plant into becoming something more, to reach its full potential. Also, why would you want a flower you couldn't smell? Being Fae isn't just about being mean, malicious, and murderous like you think. We can live forever, and it's about living life to the fullest, every moment being a new, interesting, and enjoyable experience. Have you ever wanted to experience the scent of a flower that was beautiful, but you couldn't smell it?"

"Yeah, my parents took me to Hawaii for vacation. The flowers there are beautiful. Lots of them have scents, and you can smell them like plumerias. That is my favorite—you can smell it everywhere. But some didn't smell like anything. They were pretty, but that was it. It was like they're supposed to sit on a shelf and you look at them." The grass grows up around us, and I trail my fingers across the heavy heads of wheat, twirling around in a circle. A smile steals across my face and I sneak a glance at Janice.

Janice smiles back. "I'm sure the flower had a scent so delicate you couldn't smell it, but you knew it had one and you were angry you couldn't smell it."

Tilting my head to the side to glance down as the wildflowers bloom in my wake, I swiftly reply, "Why would you say that? How can I instinctively know there should be a scent, but I can't smell it? Until I came here, I was human." I search his face for an answer.

"Are you sure about that, Sarah?" Janice whispers every word slow and deliberate.

"Yeah, my parents were married before I was born. My mother's like a crazy housekeeping nun. She'd never cheat on my father. You think she ever looked at anybody other than my dad?" I ask him.

"How can you explain her knowledge of Fae songs, especially the cleaning songs?" he remarks.

"Like, I said. she was kind of a hippie at one time, maybe she learned it from a friend." I sound weak like I'm groping for some better explanation.

"You really believe that? You really believe your mother never did anything, ever before she met your dad? He's the biggest adventure she's ever had?" Janice's questioning tone grates on me.

"I don't know. What are you trying to say?" I retort.

Janice sighs.

I continue, "My mother's not here to ask and only she knows. She likes to clean house, she's kind of boring, she hates fairies and always has. As far as I know, she's never been with anybody but my dad. So, I don't know what you're getting at."

He rushes on, "I think this is a conversation for your mother, a real conversation. Hasn't she ever done anything that would make you question her knowledge of Fae?"

Every direction I turn, a new problem pops up. Not even five minutes of peace.

"I don't want to talk about this anymore. If I want to know whether my mother knew about fairies before y'all decided to invade our lives, I'll ask her about it. Just as soon as I get back to her, okay?" Oh fuck, I made it sound like she's still alive.

He nods his head and turns his eyes away.

I could see he didn't believe me. Yeah, I'm avoiding it. It is a strange conversation, 'Hey, Mom, did you know about fairies before they landed?' If I were my mom, I'd be like 'Hell no, get away from me, you're crazy.'

"You're getting at something, something you want to say, but you don't want to say. What is it you're holding back?" I demand. "Why would you think my mom would know anything about fairies?" I hunch my shoulders and wave my hands in the air.

"Have you never heard of a changeling, Sarah?" Janice asks, standing stock still.

"Some old Irish or Scottish thing, where supposedly fairies steal people's babies and leave their own behind? The changeling is sickly, or fairies stealing babies." I shrug.

Janice is slow to reply. "That's one way of putting it. You humans are so scintillating in your definitions. There's another version of that same story, only instead of fairies changing babies out, fairies make babies with humans." He emphasizes the 'make' part.

My mouth goes dry. A fairy had a baby with a human. I don't remember them calling it a changeling, but that's really semantics. "You think I'm a changeling?" I scoff at him.

"I'm not the one saying it, you are. All I am saying is your ability to wield magic as quickly and as easily as you do is practically unheard of in the Fae world. We expected the competition to take a lot longer before anyone would develop their magic, yet you presented before the first challenge." He's frozen with arms crossed, facing away from Deston's castle of lies.

If I am a changeling that would make me half Fae. Janice glances over his shoulder. I was staring at him. He gives me a half smile. My heart turns over as my belly flips.

We aren't so different, Janice and I. I want to reach out and touch him and tell him I didn't think being part Fae would be so bad. But, how can I? His words ring true—I *am* different from the other contenders. I used magic before the first challenge.

My mother did say strange things. *'It's not a game and Fae play for keeps.'* Why would she say that?

The blood drains from my face as the pounding in my chest rises to a roar in my ears. How would she know the Fae played for keeps unless she'd met one?

I push the thought to the side. Whatever my mother does or does not know won't save my life or keep me safe. Only the black-haired Fae in front of me can help with that.

CHAPTER 14

Janice drops the subject and immediately attacks with a sword. I did my best to fight him off, but truthfully he is just a better swordsman. I did manage to make a bunch of flowers grow around him enough to make him stop. I grew a daisy-chain in an effort to hold him. The crash of metal meeting each other fills the air. It is our dance, and I want more. But then it is time to return to the castle.

"I'll go to Deston and gauge the danger. You return to your quarter's. I'll meet you there." Janice throws me a half smile and turns to the drawbridge.

Fae doesn't really have a night or day. It's their version of day, and then a long twilight where the lights never turn off, but they're not really on. Fae is safe for the most part in the day-glo light. When twilight hits, the wilder creatures come out to roam. Even though I didn't want to go back to the castle, the safety of the castle offers is important.

My steps ring in the courtyard only to be deadened by the tight quarters in the stairwell. I allow the rope to pull me up the stairwell, then I head to my room, dragging my feet every step of the way.

Janice loiters outside my door, as much as a statue can loiter. More like a Beefeater standing guard at Whitehall. All he needs is the big hat and a rifle.

"Deston informed me that arrangements had been made in my absence. You will be taught a lesson." Janice's lips are set in a grim line.

"Taught a lesson? What am I, three? Why doesn't he come to give me a spanking or stand me in a corner? Perhaps I should go sit in time out?" I huff.

"We will know soon enough what he planned. The mere fact he excludes me from his plans is telling enough. He fears his grip over his own domain. Go clean up, and I'll check back with you in one of your human hours." He extends his arm as if to touch me, his aura burns fiery red. My heart speeds up. But at the last second, he pulls his fingers back into a tight fist, then turns on one foot and strides away.

I was done with this game. I want him to touch me. I want that kiss. I imagine the burning red of his aura engulfing the white of mine. I can feel the fire of it consuming me and I close my eyes with the vision.

"My Lady, come inside," Lavender beckons me to bathe and I follow her call.

I managed to convince Lavender to let me put a shower in the bathroom. It resembles a giant flower and rains down on me the pressure sucks. But it is better than waiting for an entire bathtub to fill up every time I want to wash.

Leaving the bathroom, I come face-to-face with Lavender. "Oh, my lady, there were some men here while you were bathing. They installed something." Her lips tremble with fear.

"Installed something? Could you be any more cryptic? What are you talking about, Lavender?" I scoff at her while adjusting my towel.

"Perhaps you should open the door and see for yourself?" she replies and leads me to the door.

Lavender is skittish and frightened—that happens when you're ruled by a tyrant. But she piques my curiosity. I shrug into the bathrobe she offers. *Did he station armed guards on my door, whoopee do?* I whistle the door open—it wasn't armed guards. I am greeted by the bars of a jail cell. I reach out to push them open, only to have my skin burn upon connection with the metal. I scream out in pain. All of the skin that had come in contact with the bars reddens and blisters.

Janice's says, "You won't get out that way."

I spy Janice coming down the hall. "What is this?" I demand, cradling my injured hand to my chest.

"It's iron. Deston put an iron gate on your door. This is his punishment for defying him. It's proof that no matter what you do, he still has control here. You can't get out, and no one else can get in. Lavender's trapped there with you," Janice informs me.

"How are we supposed to eat?" I ask.

"Something will be brought to you, I'm sure, by whatever human installed this evil contraption." Janice stood some distance away from the gate. The iron wakes work on him, and he physically trembles with pain.

"I took all the humans he had, there's no human's left in the castle," I remark.

Janice shakes his head and shut his eyes.

"Sarah, you set them free. He just goes right back to the surface and collects more. You didn't really think that by taking all those kids you were saving them, did you? He might not have those specific kids, but he has a brand-new set." Janice rubs his forehead and crosses his arms. "Once you've been here for a few decades he figures you won't care about the few human slaves he's been hiding," Janice supplies.

If it was possible, I'm pretty sure there would be steam rising off of my skull. He double-crossed me, bastard. I ran the conversation over again in my mind. Nothing about our deal said he couldn't get more. I only said he had to give me the ones he had. *Stupid, stupid, stupid! I should be so much smarter than this.*

Move on to what's more important. Once I'm Queen I'll fix his wagon. "So, when's he gonna let me out of here?" As I take a step away from the bars, the wakes burn into me like the radiation of a bad sunburn.

"You will not be allowed to leave your room until the final competition. No more training, and I am the only one you are to see." I sneer at him, even though it's not Janice's fault, it's mine. Eight days, that's all I need to wait. I'd be free to roam the castle grounds right now if I'd kept my mouth shut. But he's been controlling me—kissed me! *Ugh!*

"Did he tell you I was a bad girl?" My snide comment isn't lost on Janice.

Janice replies. "Not exactly, he instructed me to explain who is the Lord and Master here. I informed him I had done that several times and you were too stubborn to listen to reason."

I snort.

Janice continues, "He won't kill you, he knows you're a contender by rights. He can't kill you or he would forfeit his own life. However, he doesn't want you to win, and he knows he can't control you. So now he's going to do the next best thing: cripple you." Janice's fist meets the wall. I jump with the unexpected impact. "Without proper training you won't survive—it's that simple, Sarah. He doesn't want you to win since he's got his eye on another contender. He's already decided if he can't control you then he at least wants one he has a chance with. You made it very clear you wouldn't tolerate his presence under your reign." His shoulders strain with pent-up irritation.

My mouth goes dry. I didn't say anything about reigns or Queens or thrones when I was around him, had I? "All I said is I won't be under his control."

Janice shakes his head and runs his fingers from top to bottom of his scalp.

"It doesn't matter. You placed yourself above him, you made it clear you see yourself above him, Sarah." He punches the wall again. "You could've just stood there and not sat in the chair. But no, you can't do that, can you? No, you had to win. You're not happy to withdraw. You're also not willing to save a fight for another day." He moves closer to the gate, and his skin reddens with the magic battering him. "When the gauntlet is thrown you must win right there on the spot, and *that* is how you will lose. You must be smarter than this. I can't get you out of there, and I wouldn't risk your life helping you. The smart move is for you to continue your training where you are." Janice punches the wall next to the bars in frustration, and I watch the magic burn the side of his hand.

My fist hits the surrounding frame to the gate. The crashing squeak of wood being crushed under my knuckles is as unsatisfying as a half sneeze. Crossing my arms, I purse my lips and slump my back into the wall.

"How the hell am I supposed to train in this dinky room?" I throw a glance over my shoulder. He leans in closer to the bars, and he whispers, "Not all fights are won with swords, Sarah. Perhaps you and Lavender can train with simple magic.

Or you can rearrange your room and train with the sword anyway. I'll do my best to stay close by, as I've been ordered to keep an eye on you." He turns his head from side to side. "Train as much as you can with magic. I'll be back later." He winks at me and turns away.

"Where are you going?" My heart jumps to my throat.

"To ask an old friend for help," He replies.

I watch as he strides away. For some stupid reason, my heart speeds up. Is he calling in a favor for me?

CHAPTER 15

Turning, I find Lavender's concerned face as she slowly pulls fibers out of a piece of fabric she'd picked up. It wasn't like her to use her hands for something when magic would have been faster.

"Well, it's a good thing I like you and we seem to get along because it looks like it's just you and me, kid." I wink at her to release some tension and put her at ease.

She lets out a nervous giggle.

"Perhaps we should follow Janice's instructions and I will show you everything I know?" Lavender returns.

My left-hand grabs the edge of the door and I slam it as hard as I can, whistling the lock home.

"Well other than hair, makeup, and clothes, do you know anything I can use in battle? At this point, I can't afford to lose." My heart clenches. *The end is near and everything that comes with it.* Reaching up, I nervously scratch my head—the bumps are larger with spiky points and my back aches. I roll my shoulders and head, stretching my arms back behind my body to loosen up.

Lavender picks up two vials and sets them on the receiving table. I perched on the edge of the bed.

I smile, rubbing my hands together. "Show me what you can do."

Lavender waves her hands over the vials, both float up as she sings a quick ditty, then shoots them across the room. One explodes next to the window and the other lay on the ground, benignly rolling from side to side.

"Exploding glass vials?" I exclaim.

"Yes, my lady. They don't seem dangerous, but once you use the energy potion inside, all you're left with is the glass, so don't waste a potential weapon." Her solemn reply shakes me. "Everything you take into the next challenge, you need to use to your advantage. Even if it's as simple as a glass vial or stopper."

I smirk at her. "What the hell is a stopper going to do? I get making the glass explode since shards flying everywhere can cause pain," I say, waving to indicate the glass bits embedded in the wall.

"You can use magic to force a stopper to fly down someone's throat and maybe choke them. If they can't sing, they can't save themselves. Not all Fae are capable of humming their magic, or in your case letting it reverberate from your chest. They can't make those deep sounds they have to sing or whistle. If you can choke them, you take away their ability to make magic." She shrugs a shoulder.

Further proof all Fae are vicious killers, even the ones that make you dress up pretty. I like Lavender's simplicity. Her magic doesn't require some special ability. You simply use what you had available. Lavender's idea of self-defense isn't sexy, but it is effective.

"Have you ever used it on anyone?" I float over a vial from the vanity and thrust it at the wall, humming the explosion before impact.

Shaking her head, she glances down. "No, my lady, I don't fight duels, but I can dress you for one." We both burst out laughing.

"Well, if I'm going to duel, I definitely want to look good, so I'll keep that in mind. Okay, what else do you have?" I search the room for our next makeshift weapon.

"If we go on the premise that everything is a weapon, then you must simply figure out how to use it. We could start talking about how I put your hair up again. Also, jewelry—jewelry is an effective weapon," she yammers on.

I listen to Lavender expound on the various attributes of how clothing can be used to choke someone to death or trap them, and that hair actually can be turned into its own rope, then returned to its natural shape. She shows me how I can dismantle the buckles with a whistle and turn them around and restrain someone.

"So, what gives? You moved two vials, but you only blew one up why not the other?" I point at the innocuous-looking vial on the grounds.

She returns a shy smile. "Yes, I was wondering how long you would allow it to sit there before questioning its presence. Actually, that vial isn't anything more than poison."

I raise an eyebrow at her. "Poison, why is it in here?"

"Poison can be just as effective at killing your enemies. Especially if you get it down their throat. Many Fae take a deep breath and open their mouth wide before they sing a difficult spell. All you need to do is pull the stopper and dump it down their throat." She finishes.

"Have you used this yourself?" I demand.

She shakes her head. "No, but I have seen other Fae do it. Before the old Queen vanished, there was a young and handsome Seelie prince the Queen favored. One of the UnSeelie princes was jealous of him. One day they went on a hunt, for at his heart the Seelie prince was a hunter. The jealous prince claimed to have seen a white stag and invited the Queen and her court to come along for the hunt. During the chase, the Seelie Prince killed the stag and died." Tears glisten in her eyes. She must have known the guy.

"Who was this handsome prince?" I inquire softly.

"He was my brother. He wasn't in love with the Queen. He had been in love with someone else, but she left him. She was a changeling, they can never choose one world over the other. They are always trapped between the two." She looks away and her shoulders shudder as she wanders into the bathroom.

"He was good?" I want to follow her, but I didn't want to intrude. The Fae run around half-clothed, but then you see them get emotional and they are truly naked.

"He was a prince of the Seelie court. He had beautiful jet-black hair like yours. At that time, I was Seelie too. But after he died I changed— I was angry." She offers up her defense too quickly.

Her sadness colors her aura. A deep gray moves out from her gripping me. She always seems so happy and light, as if most things don't bother her. It was all an act, however, another fake pretty Fae face hiding the dirty truth.

She misses her brother and is angry over it, so angry she switched courts, crazy. I whistle the broken glass vial away into the wall, and the wood absorbs its energy. Fae recycling is fascinating to watch. If only recycling on the surface was so easy.

"Lavender, do you want to talk about your brother?" I inquire

"I think about him a great deal, but it was long ago. He didn't even want to be the Queen's consort— the other Fae was jealous. The princes fight amongst themselves constantly," she muses.

"Which one of the princes killed him?" I hold my breath.

She meets my eyes and stills. "You can't guess?" she asks, quirking an eyebrow at me.

A gasp escapes my throat. How can she stay here and look at that man if he killed her brother? "Why are you here?" I demand.

"I told you a long time ago my services are expensive, and I was brought here for you. Originally, I was with Jacques the other UnSeelie prince. He loaned me out." Lavender smiles it is grim.

"How can you stand to be near the man that killed your brother? Showing him polite respect while knowing what he did?" I wave my hand at the door as if it would make Deston appear.

"I am right where I need to be. I am on loan, by choice. Jacques could never make me come here if I didn't wish it. After all, you need me." She glances down, then gazes up at me through her bangs. She changes her hair color from green to blue in the blink of an eye, batting her matching blue lashes.

There was more to Lavender, and for the first time, I got the feeling she was hiding something. She presses her lips into a straight line and busies herself as far from the door as possible.

CHAPTER 16

I practice changing mundane items into weapons, or at the very least something to protect myself with until the fairy light dims outside.

"Lavender, what time does the light fade?" I watched as the Fae day turned to the black-light type of night.

"About supper time." She looks around expectantly, her eyes landing briefly on the door.

"Perhaps we should open the door, maybe we will hear them coming?" I get up and whistled the common musical combination for the lock. Hearing it click through the door, I open it to the radiating heat of the iron bars. I don't remember them being so hot before.

The ring around my head aches, as do my shoulders and spine. No matter how far I stepped back, I couldn't seem to shake the radiating power of the bars—they reached into the room, clawing at me.

"Do you feel them?" I let my fingers play across my temples, rubbing lightly and hoping that the pain would subside.

"The bars? If I go closer to the doorway I feel them. Why?" Lavender quirked an eyebrow at me.

She had to be wondering why I ask, as I'm practically next to the window.

"I can feel them even over here," I reply.

She stands up and walks next to the door, closely examining all the bars and being careful not to touch them. Then, she turned her back on them quickly.

"They don't look any different than the dungeon iron," she remarks.

"The dungeon? Why would you know what the bars in the dungeon look like?" I squeak.

Lavender quickly replies, "After you made your grand exit at the maze I was punished for a little while. They thought perhaps I'd given you something or taught you something." Her gaze is steady and emotionless.

I gasp. "They tortured you?"

"Yes, but don't worry, I didn't tell them anything. I would never tell 'him' anything. I would rather be forced into the sea and slowly chewed apart piece by piece by a Kelpie," she stands stock still, "Then help 'him' with anything." Her whole countenance darkens as her nose curls up on one side. Even her aura changes to a darker color. Instead of the bright pink she usually flaunts, it turns to a dark fuchsia almost bloody.

"I'm so…" I break off, swallowing the apology with the bile. "Did they actually touch you with the iron?"

"My lady, don't worry about what they did or didn't do to me in the dungeon. These bars are no different, and you can survive them. You must simply stay away from them. The real question is, whatever shall we do for dinner?" She smiles brightly, changing the subject.

"You don't think they're coming, do you?" I swallow.

Heaving a sigh, she replies, "No, my lady, they are not coming. As a matter of fact, his Grace must have ordered the water turned off. But I filled the tub up a while ago." I gasp. I didn't realize the length Deston was willing to go to. He intends for me to die here?

Fat chance on that. I stand up and look around at the walls, all of them bloom with flowers. You can't eat flowers, or could you? Flowers are the precursors of fruit.

My eyes follow the line of the trees in the room. The pieces of wood, branch or vine, they've intertwined themselves into the castle walls, creating the very structure we stand upon.

Nothing is stopping me from force-growing food. Reverberation begins in my chest, and I focus on one of the flowers, altering it. I picture in my mind what I know an orange blossom looks like prior to fruit. Slowly, the blossom reforms itself and begins to fruit, as do several others around it. Lavender claps her hands.

"Oh, my lady, I have never witnessed anyone change a flower. You actually made it fruit."

"No, I didn't, I asked it to be fruit and told it what kind I like." My satisfied reply wakes out, the room itself-morphs in keeping with my desires.

"Can you teach me how to do that?" Lavender asks. I thought about the only song with fruit in it. Something I'd heard as a young child. A song about fruit salad. I hum it out loud to her and tell her to picture fruit salad. A moment later, one entire wall turns into a bower of tropical fruits, grapes, bananas, and cherries. There were even a few apples.

Lavender laughs. "I have never sung a fruit basket song." Her glee is infectious, but it reminded me again how easy it would be for someone to misuse this ability. Just because you can sing something into existence doesn't mean that you're going to do good with it.

I taught Lavender how to make a fruit salad from a wall. Yet not even 30 minutes ago she was teaching me to strangle someone to death and encumber their arm with hair so I could control their weapon.

The soft tread of footsteps drifts down the hall. I run to the door in anticipation of Janice's return, only to be met by a kid with milky-white, entranced eyes. His clothes are filthy and torn. He couldn't have been more than fifteen, and he carries a light shadow of a beard and an ivory scroll.

I watch him slip the ivory scroll through the iron bars, and it falls to the floor with a light thump.

"His Grace, UnSeelie Prince Deston of the Fae Realm, bids me deliver this message to you." He turns and retraces his steps down the hall.

The burning on my face is not an unfamiliar feeling. I snatch up the scroll and step back. I didn't need to relive my scars.

I break the reddish wax seal and unroll the paper.

Submit to me and he lives. You have two days.

My hands crush the edges of the scroll as the liquid jet fuel of adrenaline races through my veins. Who did he mean? Janice? Arty? Who is 'he'? I choke on the bitter taste. It doesn't matter which one he had, I couldn't let either die. Arty is my best friend and brother and Janice my...

I had to be honest with myself, Janice isn't just my ally or vassal, friend or adviser, but there is something more. There could be more, I want more. Tears threaten, along with a lump that fills in my throat.

What if he made me choose?

I've never known true fear. I'd been scared before, many times. But this causes terror to quake in my bones. I can't choose, ever. I'd rather die.

How dare he threaten me. My body shakes with rage fueled by fear and the certain knowledge Deston cannot be allowed to win.

I will never bow to Deston.

I slam the door on the iron and the little pieces of paper resembling confetti on the floor of the hall.

Pain radiating from the iron bars burns and pulls my skin. Things between Lavender and I ground to a halt. I think I'd reached the highest level of her expertise. She is inventive and imaginative but I'm afraid not a lot of practical combat experience.

As much as I want to close the door, I can't. I thirst for contact with the outside world. I am trapped in my room, with the walls closing in on me. I'm sure a lot of prisoners feel that way. People don't really sympathize much with them: how much punishment it really is to be imprisoned. From what Lavender intimated, I guess it could be a whole lot worse. Nonetheless, I hold my sword and practice my footwork. I hack the wardrobe apart five times and whistled it back together, then sheathe Silver and go to look out the window. In two days, my imprisonment would be over, along with perhaps everything else. The day-glo flailing light glistens off the surfaces, shooting iridescent rainbows across what little I can see of Deston's domain.

"My lady, can we please close the door?" Lavender's request comes out more like a plea. I notice she is retreating to the far corner of the room, desperate to get away from the waking pain. I nod my head—there is no point keeping it open. Janice isn't coming.

There were only two days left, I had yet to ask the question why. Why did Janice help me, it can't just be because he thought I am their best chance? That rings untrue to me, there is something else, I know there is. Of course, trying to whittle away the truth from the lies is always difficult when you're dealing with a race of pathological liars.

Is he a liar? Did he ever really lie to me? Maybe he just told me what I needed to hear.

CHAPTER 17

No one came, not Janice, not the human boy, no one. No matter how many times I try to create a new door or entrance so we can leave, the walls won't budge. Had I caused his death or Arty's? It ate at me.

I stare at the window, pulling the vibrations from my chest and pushing the magic wake out to the crystalline glass. I watch as the panes rattled and warp, but won't break. The only change is their shape. The haphazard, mismatched shapes are now all aligned orderly rectangles. They resembled my bedroom window at home, on the surface.

Lavender's voice breaks through to me. "My lady, these walls were all built by Deston. I'm sure they like you, but they will never turn on their maker. Train, win, then you can strip Deston of all he has." I turn away from the familiar-shaped glass and take in the state of my quarters.

"She's right, these walls will never turn on their prince." I whirl around, and there leaning against the wall in black skin-tight leather pants missing a shirt stands Puca, bulging pecs and all.

"How did you get in?" I demand.

He chuckles and scratches the back of his head. "I am not constrained by the normal rules of Fae. I am neither ruled by a Queen or Wyld. I am a force unto myself." He laughs.

I watch him strut across the room, fingering the various cloth laying around. His nostrils flare, and he smacks his lips together as if tasting the air.

Puca's deep baritone rebounds off the walls. "You really should clean up, a liege should look the part."

I gasp. "What are you talking about?" I sputter.

"Oh don't play coy with me, Sarah. You finally made your choice. No more sitting on the proverbial fence, hey?" He smiles with gleaming white teeth.

I open my mouth, but he waves my protests off. "Janice came to me seeking a favor." Puca chuckles. "I granted it, little did he know I was on my way here all along. I can't let you not have a fighting chance." He stops pacing in front of the wardrobe door—it hangs at an odd angle. I had almost removed it from the cabinet *practicing*.

"Me?" I let the question hang in the air.

"You ask too many questions; it's not good for royalty to not know all the answers. The wisest sit quietly and listen. Eventually, a Fae will tell you everything you want to know. Now, I'm going to take Lavender to my home. She has played her part and it is over for now." He extends his right hand to her. Lavender bounces up and lays her hand over his.

My mouth dries with the length of time I've let it hang open. "My Lady, I had planned to stay till the end. If I stay 'he' will use me against you. I won't be an impediment." She pats my arm. "I know we will meet again."

Turning, she smiles to Puca, and the air around them shimmers and splits. They step through to a cozy room on the other side.

I move to join them, but the magic closes in my face. I'm left to gaze around the room alone.

Great.

My back itches terribly, The bumps bulge out, and a thought occurs to me it is the first time in weeks I'm alone.

Pulling my shirt off, along with my sports bra, I whistle up the mirror.

The face looking back at me is the face of a scarred alien. My fingers trail over the partially melted skin on my right side. The few drops from the unicorn had healed a small part of my ear and cheek. But it did nothing for the drooping skin over my eye or the missing hair. Droplet-shaped scars dapple my upper chest and part of one breast. I clutch my shirt to my chest.

I turn to my good side and pretend it is my whole face. Heat burns behind my eyes, and in my nose.

Stop, Sarah! It is, what it is, and it will be what it will be. You can't change the past. I hum the back mirror into being and examine the two growths on my back. They lay on either side of my spine, between my shoulder blades. I move my arms and the bulge ripples with movement. I gasp in shock.

I lift one arm, reaching for the sky, and the corresponding bump moves in an upward fashion. I pull my arm down and whistled both mirrors away.

I squeeze my eyes shut to wish the monstrous sight from my mind. But no amount of darkness could erase the vision.

Fae is ruining me, distorting everything about me. I grind my teeth.

"It's okay, I'll wait for you to change," Puca's deep timber reverberates around the room. I throw a glance over my shoulder and see his muscled back. I scramble back into my sports bra and slip my shirt over my head. Then I belt Silver back around my waist, allowing it to rest on my hips.

"You can turn around and explain yourself." I cross my arms and cock a hip out.

Puca throws his head back and bellows, "I never explain myself to anyone. But spoken like a true Queen.' He claps his hands in a mocking manner.

"I must say I wasn't sure you would choose Fae. But I am glad. Where to begin? This isn't exactly what I had planned, but you are as unpredictable as I am." Puca says, then he reaches out as if to touch the side of my face.

I step back out of reach.

"I won't hurt you, Sarah. I would never hurt my..." Puca's smile fades away, and he presses his lips together.

"What did you say, your what?" I scoff at him. He reaches for me again and I slap his hand away.

"Well, quick and dirty it is." He pauses to take a breath and plunges back in. "I'm here to finish training you, so you can win and end this cycle of death." He steps around me and whispers in my ear, "The rule of wild must come to an end." He double steps around the room several times in a circle. I turn, following his moves, but I find words don't come to mind.

"Cat got your tongue? This isn't a game, and Fae play for keeps." Puca's reply sounds familiar—I'd heard that exact statement before, from my mother. I shake my head, stay on target.

"Janice, where is he? Deston sent me a note implying he had him, or Arty," I demand.

"Oh, was it a note or a threat?" Puca fingers his goatee then crosses and uncrosses his arms, flexing all of his muscles at the same time.

"It was a threat, submit or else. But I don't know if it's Janice or Arty that he plans to kill." My eyes finally meet his. They are yellow like a cat, but I saw them red as fire when he became the black horse. He cocks one eyebrow at me, with a half-smile distorting his handsome face. I cock the same brow, mirroring him minus the smile.

"Can we begin?" he inquires, then trails his finger across the bed's duvet cover.

"What about Deston's threat?" I can't let it go. Arty or Janice's safety depends on what Deston did. The butterflies in my chest beat at me, keeping me awake and worried.

Puca waves his hand around dismissively. "He wouldn't dare kill whoever he thinks he has. Jacques has Arthur —do you think he would trade such a valuable person to his rival? Put your mind at rest. Deston is playing on your fears, don't fall for his shenanigans." Puca slicks his thick curls back from his forehead. All at once, he shivers. I watch as every hair on his body moves like a wave. I'd only ever seen a horse do that.

I did breathe easier, though not because I trust or necessarily believe Puca, but because of his logic. Deston would be a fool to kill anyone I care about, and Jacques is not foolish enough to trade away leverage. Perhaps they're both safe. I hope.

"You have weapons, so let's test them." Puca pulls a sword from the air and whips it around, all the while morphing the room into an empty space.

I attack first but he easily deflected my blows.

Puca yawned. "Come now, Sarah, you fight like Janice. That will never do. You favor your right side. I think your vision is weak on that side, that won't do one bit." He shakes his head while making a tsk-tsk sound.

I bristle at his flippant comment. I don't care who he is, my looks are off limits. Puca taps his lips with an index finger and sings a ditty under his breath. I watch as the wakes rush to my skin.

Then I arch up on to my tiptoes in agony. The next wake of magic moves over me, bending me in half, releasing a scream. The power of his magic pounds me, making me lose my grip on Silver. The blade clatters to the floor and I crumple next to it. The right side of my body burns in agony as I roll over onto my back to strain in torment.

"Just a little more, my child, then we can start again," Puca's deep baritone moves over my skin, tearing it to shreds. I squeeze my eyes shut to clear away the black spots clouding my vision. All I can feel is the painful magic washing over my tender flesh, cutting it into a thousand pieces then sewing it back together. I pant with each wake, dark spots shine before my eyes. His song rises, bringing a new level of torment and spasms.

I ache with his song. The new sounds bring new magic beating at my physical being. The air around me vibrates with magic. It harmonized over me pushing and pulling, ripping and tearing at my skin, knitting and smoothing. At one point I swear the tip of a knife slices my shoulder open, filleting the dead and scarred flesh away. Just when I think it will end, a new refrain begins along with a new affliction.

I pant with each beat of my heart, turning from one side to the other seeking an easy place to rest. Over the last few months I'd accumulated scars in so many places there was no ease to be found.

My hands curled into tight balls, digging nails into tender skin. Sometime later, the pain and song reverberate away, carrying the lion's share of the misery with it.

Puca pushes my hair back from my face. "Rest, Sarinah, I'll return with food and practice for the real fight."

I move my lips to reply, but words won't come. Soft lips press to my forehead. I breathe in the musky scent of horse and man, only to find it all at once gone. I am alone again. Sleep overwhelms me, and I embrace it.

CHAPTER 18

Peeling back my eyes is like peeling the sticky label on a jar, slow and painstaking. Even after I open them, the adhesive film still clings to the back of my lids. I'm lying on a bed in my room.

"Oh good, you're awake. I have food, so eat up because there is much to do and little time to do it. You slept longer than I anticipated. We have little more than a Fae day." Puca hops out of his chair and saunters to the pristine wardrobe yanking the door open to reveal the inside of a fridge.

"What the fuck did you do to me?" I ask rubbing the sleep from my eyes and pushing the hair out of my face. My hands freeze midway across my face. The sensation of pushing hair over my right ear, a full ear, sends tingles across fresh new skin that has never been touched before. I inspect every facet of my face like a blind person, sliding my hand over both sides at the same time. My right eye is no longer partially covered by sagging melted skin. Instead firm, skin with a delicate eyebrow lines the outer edge. The wrenched skin on my cheek is smoothed into high-boned perfection, leaving a hollow just below the bone.

The warmth created by my new hair comforts me—you don't realize how much you love something until it's gone. I love my hair, all of it. I love the way it cascades down my back. When a cold breeze brought shivers and goosebumps to my skin, I could rearrange my hair to warm my ears, neck, and shoulders. Heat burns behind my eyes, threatening to spill the tears welling up there. The need to cry pressed on my chest. I don't care what Janice said. I want a good cry, I need one.

The walls ran with moisture and wake with joy reflecting my mood. I whistle the mirror into existence. It reveals what my hands found. I am whole, and the disfiguring scar covering the right side of my face trailing down my neck to my breast is gone. The skin fresh and opalescent, glowing with the light of Fae. My Fae markings are in full bloom over my skin. For it is still twilight outside.

Light green dots arche over my eyes, and go down and around to the edge of my cheeks. Long thin lines run from the last dot to my collar bone and swirl to my shoulders. Even the patchy burn marks on my legs are gone.

"You healed me?" Disbelief colors my voice.

"Of course I healed you. How that animal could have left you that way is unfathomable. You are my progeny, and I would never leave you disfigured. It was never my intent for any of this to happen." Puca's normal devil-may-care act was discarded. I now see the real man inside. His ancient eyes tell a story of untold suffering and loss.

I explode. "But you have to care to heal."

"It's easy to care about one's flesh and blood. It isn't care, it's love. You have to love to heal. Who's been training you?" He scoffs and crosses his arms.

"That is a lie. I've healed and I didn't love, I barely cared," I whisper.

"The rule of magic doesn't change for anyone. If you healed, you loved. It took me a long time to heal you. Someone tried healing you before, but they botched the job." He paces the room like a caged animal, examining the walls and flaring his nostrils. The motion reminds me of a dog in a kennel. His every move is instinctive and primal.

"Don't talk about Janice like that. He didn't botch it, he just couldn't finish without revealing me to Deston. Janice did it to save my life, I was dying." I jump up, the healing giving me renewed vigor. My sword lay on the floor, but a hum later it is in my hand and raised against Puca.

"I love it when you're mad. Don't let it rule you, Sarinah." He moves so fast it registers as a blur, and suddenly I am on my back.

All the air in my chest pushed out with the impact. "Stop calling me that!" I growl and lift my legs up before using the momentum to leap into the air. I've never been able to do that before.

"You take well to Fae, Sarinah. Your blood makes mushrooms, does it not?" Puca queries while standing over me.

"You know it does, everyone does. How do you know my real name?" I hold my sword aloft in readiness.

"I gave it to you. Easy to remember something you chose. The past is irrelevant. It's what's to come that matters. Tell me about yourself and show me your abilities." He leans back against a wall and crosses both legs and arms, then gives me a wink.

"Do the Fae even know how to tell the truth? My mother named me, not you," I growl, sidestepping around one of the chairs in the room. I dart a glance around. Puca already warped the bed back into the wall, leaving only the chair and a small side table with a cup of water.

"Your changeling mother didn't name you. She gave me that honor, as she should. Do you know why the Fae go through this ridiculous ritual every few thousand years? Because no one will listen to me." He sighs and calls a sword to him, slamming it against mine.

"Don't change the subject with your Fae lies. How do you know my name? No one calls me that, or even knows it." My heart beats through my chest. My mother was very insistent I not tell anyone my real name. My fingers tighten on the hilt and I return the blow. The crashing of metal on metal ring out its own tune, tickling my ears and throwing sharp wakes at the walls, only to reverberate back at us.

"Ha, good girl, but you have a tell. Your hands grip tighter before you attack. You must learn to control that. Again!" Puca's call for action is backed by an attack. He whirls the blade around and smacks me on the ass with the flat of the blade.

"You bastard!" Heat pours from my head. I raise Silver and slash down at him, but he dances away on tiptoes with glee.

"You'll have to do better than that. Also, Fae can't be bastards we are born of magic, not parents. I have one beginning from one Queen." His eyes flash with mischievousness and a one-eyed wink as he whirls his sword over the back of his hand.

I huff with irritation, lunging forward with a skipping step, but he whirls around and smacks my butt. Losing my balance, I tumble forward. I tuck my head under and roll head over heels. Twisting like a snake onto my belly I use the momentum to jump into a crouching position and slash at his calves.

He leaps to the side, laughing at my feeble attempts to down him. I plant the tip of my blade into the floor for leverage and take to my feet.

Yanking Silver from the floor, I whistle the chair from across the room and slam it into Puca. His feet lift into the air and he lands on his back, coughing out a laugh.

"Oh, this is fun. But we need to move on to the hard stuff." In a flash, he's off the floor and slashing at me. I barely have time to raise Silver and deflect his blows.

"You don't move fast enough. The princes will throw all of Fae and wild at you before they let you sit on the stone throne. All who benefit from the rule of wild are aligned against you. You need to learn all my tricks to survive." Puca's eyes align with mine, the golden hue hard as a canary diamond. He holds my sword locked in a crossed embrace, one quillion over the other.

"How do you move so fast?" I pant out, straining against him.

Puca replies, "I don't think of where I'm going. I see myself there already." A second later he is across the room, leaning against the wall one foot crossed over the other.

I stumble forward with his withdraw.

"The magic will bend to your will if you show it what you want." Once again, he is standing by my side with my sword in his hand.

"Don't think! See!" Puca throws his hip into mine. I see myself standing on the other side of the room, and I am suddenly there with my back to Puca and stumbling from the hip-thrust.

The slapping of two hands together echoes around the room, bouncing from one wall to the other. "You learn quick. That's good since we don't have much time. Next lesson, how to get out of here."

Puca's eyes change to green and a real smile plays on his lips. I see my Fae self reflected in his face, along with shades of my mother. We have to share blood.

CHAPTER 19

Both our faces curved back into reflective smiles. "Show me!" I order.

"You understand intent, yes?" Puca locks both thumbs into the loops on his leather pants, then strolls across the room to look out the window. Freeing one hand, he runs a finger across one of the crystal panes. "Looks as though you're close…" Puca turns to face me. "Very close. This window carries surface traces. Did you do this?" His eyes search my face for the answer he already had.

"I tried to remove the window, but now it looks like my old bedroom window. I spent at least an hour on that," I reply and cross my arms defensively.

"Close, oh so close. What were you thinking when this happened?" Puca dances around the information. Is this how all of Fae teaches: ask a question and wait for the pupil to figure it out? *Why can't it be like cooking?* Add two cups of flour and one third of a cup of oil, a little sugar, butter, and voila, cake?

"I wanted to open the wall so we could float out. I was going to turn a chair into a platform and leave. I wanted to leave this room," I retort.

"Your thoughts of 'home' on the surface cloud you. Push it away. I promise, when you win, we will return to the surface for your mother." His piercing gaze leaves no question of the truth behind his words.

"My mother is dead." I lock my jaw down on the lie as the butterflies begin swooping around in my belly.

Puca threw his head back and barks out a laugh. "Your mother is safe and sound in the basement of a house down the street from your old home. I know because I put her there, along with that man she loves." He opens and closes his mouth, dryly smacking his lips in distaste. I gasp at his revelation.

"You, you put them there?" I sputter.

He waves his hand in that, oh-so-irritating Fae fashion of dismissal. "Of course. You don't think Janice and his cohorts would have let them live without my intervention, do you? My only regret was your early exit. I was late, both times."

"Both times?" Toddler questions again.

"Yes, I meant to retrieve you that first night, but you'd already been spotted. I had to wait. Deston has watched me for centuries looking for Alice."

My thoughts run wild with his information dump. Wracking my brain, I dig back to that first night. I thought I saw a horse, but it had only been a shadow.

"You were down the other alleyway from me? The black horse. Why were you coming for us?" I step back, bracing myself for a fight as my heart rate picks up.

Puca sighs and runs his fingers through his black curls, then shakes his head in a horse-like fashion. "I promised Alice I would come for her and the baby when the Queen was dead. I was going to take you and train you myself. But I was too late, and Janice found you first. I put your mother somewhere safe and went looking for you. Without a magic trail to follow you made it difficult. The past isn't important, however, you need to move forward. Focus on the task at hand: winning." He waves his hand over the window, and it shivers and splits.

The wakes move out from a circular opening in the wall to reveal my old room.

Puca steps to the side with an inviting arm. "Do you want to go here?" His thumb pushes off his index finger and snaps the room away. The portal now opens onto Sorensen's kitchen. "Or perhaps here? We could greet my daughter and be on our way." He cocks an eyebrow at me with a half-smile.

"Or perhaps you prefer this one." His fingers snap again. There, huddled on the stone floor, sits Janice covered in blisters. He lifts his head enough to crack a swollen eye at us.

Leaping through the portal, I land at his side. I plant both hands on either side of his face and lift his limp head. Misshaped bruises color his reddened skin, caused by the heat emanating from the metal behind me.

I whip my head back to the portal. Puca stands on the other side, his face barely registering a thought or feeling.

"If you want to come back, you will need intent. Don't think it, see it." The portal slams closed, a gruff laugh echoing in the background.

Agh. "You Fucking Bastard." My scream echoes around the cell, bouncing from one wall to the other.

Turning my ire inward, I search Janice's face.

"Are you okay? What can I do to make it better?" I inquire.

Janice's eyes roll around in his head, and his muscles flex with pain. I examine the walls and door, they all wake with iron. The stones have reddish veins running through them, a telltale sign of raw iron ore. The door is held together with iron brackets, rivets, and screws. The entire door frame is an unbroken iron band with hinges built into the surrounding the stone opening.

The burning heat from the poisonous mineral bores into my back, leeching away my strength.

"You should leave me here and return. Puca will help you win." Janice coughs, and his lips crack, blue blood is scabbed at the edges of his eyes.

I gaze around the cell. Small fungi grow in haphazard places, some fresh and fragrant, others withered dry husks. As I touch a fingertip to a small mushroom, it disintegrates to nothing more than dust.

Lifting Janice's face in-line with mine, I choke out, "You know I can't leave you here. Deston said he'd kill you. This cell will kill you." I rub my thumb back and forth across his reddened jaw, searching for something—rejuvenation, maybe.

Janice's full lips pull back to a weak smile. "You didn't submit, did you?"

I crack a smile with trembling lips. "You should know me better than that. I'll never bow to him, not if I can win." My eyes roam over his face, hoping for something more.

His eyes lock with mine. "Leave me here, go back, train, live, and save us all. Please, Sarah, I'm just one life. Think of all the others—Arty is still alive. Win and save him."

My heart speeds up, and my smartass reply clogs my throat. "No, you aren't just one life. … if I lose you like I lost Nick. I… I can't give you up too. Who would I be if I didn't at least try?" I falter, and my teeth close on my lower lip. I can't say the three little words, I just can't.

I push the hair back from his brow, and it reveals cracked and oozing skin. The blood follows his hairline, leaking into his ears. I lean over and kiss his forehead, breathing in the scent I'd come to know so well, grassy vetiver and spice. His fingers are blackened with iron exposure, looking no different than when I'd first healed him. A pressure forms inside me.

Deston can't win, he can never win. Tearing my eyes from Janice, I pull back. This isn't going to get us out of here.

Coming to my full height, I turn, searching the weakest chink in the wall. All the wakes scream back at me. Deston had chosen well. This cell was impenetrable. A normal Fae would never be capable of escaping. Craning my neck, I take in the ceiling; it's a good 30 feet above with only two wood beams crossing the open area. Both beams wake back iron. Deston had worked it into every square inch. *Damn him.*

Janice lays on the floor with the iron beating at him. My own skin gains a pinkish hue in reaction to our surroundings. The iron will work its way into my system, weakening me the same way it had him. The longer I stay, the higher my chances of losing.

Don't think, see. A vision of my old bedroom bloomed in my mind. That is what I pictured before I changed the window and my mind. *Where had I gone wrong?* I keep staring at the walls, hoping the stones will change. My desire is for my surrounding to morph, perhaps tearing the stones open.

Magic wakes beat the iron rhythm into my flesh, sapping my strength and cooking my tender extremities. Blinking away the aching heat, I steal one last glance at Janice's prone form.

See. Raising my hand, the picture I bring to mind is of the wooden tub with the daisy showerhead raining cool water in Deston's castle. Power blasts from my palm, tearing a portal hole in the stony wall. I whistle Janice's form into a floating lump and push him through with me. The portal slams shut behind us, cutting us off from the power of the iron wakes.

I dash into the main room only to find it empty. *Puca, you asshole.* Surveying the vacant space, I find nothing. Not a note or hint of where that duplicitous, pointy-eared equine went.

I return to the washroom and Janice's floating form. He can't stay here. Where can I take him to keep him safe?

Nowhere, the world holds no safe places. Pulling the vision of my old bedroom, I allow it to fill my mind's eye. Picturing the light-filled window again, I lift my hand and press my intent into the world around me. The space in front of me rips open a shimmering portal and I drag Janice through behind me.

The sun is up and beaming through the glass panes. Instinctively my arm arches over my face for protection. Janice groans in pain. I picture myself by the window and find myself there in a flash. I yank the curtain closed, but the oppressive sun finds its way through cracks, the radiation sending out crushing wakes.

"We can't stay here," Janice whispers. I move to his side as he slumps to the floor.

"Can you stand? I'll take us anywhere you feel is safe," I whisper back while listening to my old home and all its little sounds for trouble.

Janice labors over his reply. "Puca, take us to Puca. He's the only one strong enough." He pants with pain, the sun working almost as fast as the iron.

"He's the one who left me in that cell with you. Why would I trust him again?" I scoff.

"The Fae way of teaching is by fire. Live or die, whatever power you have, you earn. How did we get here?" Janice's swollen eyes take in our surroundings.

"I opened a portal, something Puca was trying to teach me," I reply, coughing. I can't take much more of the solar radiation.

"You opened a portal? Only Puca can travel this way-how is that possible?" Awe laces his voice.

I whistle the comforter over the window, hoping the extra barrier would protect us. I arrive back at Janice's side in time to stop his fall to the floor.

"Take me to Puca, he'll keep you safe." Janice's head lolls to the side and onto my shoulder. "Do you trust me?" he whispers.

His breath skimmed my lips, and I turn into it. The sensitive flesh at the end of my nose brushes against his. My eyes find his violet orbs eating into me. The heat from the sun pales into the background as fire from my belly sweeps through me. My heart pounds in time with the heart I find under my hand.

"I trust you," I barely breathe those three difficult words.

His hand snakes behind my neck, pulling me to his warm lips. My eyes close as I melt into his embrace, exposing my longing for him as if it was an open wound.

His lips work over mine, down my jawline to the hollow of my neck. A moan escapes before his lips find mine again. I return every demand, with one of my own.

I am molten lava, hot and fast moving. But not all of the heat is my own, and the real burning inferno of the world radiates into us. Janice's hands find the small of my back and move down to the swell of my buttocks pulling me to him as his mouth works over my throat.

Janice pulls away, laying a kiss on my forehead. "We must leave, the sun will kill us if we stay much longer above ground." Anguish laces his husky voice.

"Five minutes, I only want five minutes to enjoy this moment" I whisper back. Then my lips find his and our lovers dance begins again. I move with him our hands finding each other. I want to stay in this moment with the fire of the sun burning all our problems away.

My lips still and I snuggle into the hollow of his neck breathing in the scent of him. Janice's knee's give out and I struggle to hold him upright.

"I guess it's time to go." His voice is thick and labored.

I thrust my hand out in front of me. There before us is Puca's barn, along with a few horses lingering about.

"When did you decide?" Janice inquires.

"When I saw your burnt hands. You injured yourself for me. You trusted me, the rest is a river in Egypt." I pull him back into a standing position. Biting my lip, I stumble over my words. "What about you?"

He smiles. "When I saw you jump the first fence. You were fearless. Even after missing the second fence and I pulled you lose tearing your pants, you never gave up the fight. You saw the odds and never backed down, defiant to the core and beautiful."

I pull us through to stand in front of Puca's barn.

The slapping of skin meets us.

"Awe, good girl. I see you even brought your friend." Puca's twinkling, canary-colored eyes finish the picture of arrogance that made the man. He sashays from the paddock post to stand in front of us.

"You're an asshole. You left us there knowing full well what would happen if I couldn't get out." I raise my hand to smack him, but he catches my wrist and holds it in a vise grip.

"Fae don't teach the human way. You will learn or die. What do you think the challenges are about? We are teaching you. Life is not safe; I cannot and will not coddle you. There is too much at stake. You are not the only one with something of value to lose. No matter what choice I make there will be a loss," Puca's yellow eyes glow with a sun-like brilliance.

Our faceoff does Janice no good as he slumps against me. Puca whistles and one of his horses canter over.

"This is Horatio," Puca informs me, all the while running his fingers up and down the diamond between the big hazel eyes. "Horatio will take Janice to my home, where he will be safe." Then Puca hums a ditty, placing Janice on the stallion's back.

Janice leans over and our lips meet for a quick kiss.

Puca pats Horatio on his hindquarters and the horse moves away with

Puca holding my arm, keeping me in check. I flash him a fierce snarl.

"Trust me, granddaughter. He will be safe. We must return before you are missed. They will bring you one final meal. Tomorrow begins the race to the throne." Puca releases my arm, only to shove me through a new portal.

The hardwood floor meets my ass, bruising my tailbone. I hop up into a fighting stance. Puca steps through, waving me off.

"Stop doing that and maybe I could get five minutes to trust you," I grumble.

"Don't leave the confines of this room. Deston will be alerted to your status. Only the princes know where the final race will be held, so only they can take you there. Deston must arrive with you." He waltzes around the room and bathroom only to shift on his heels by the window. Gazing into the dimming twilight of Fae, I watch as his Fae marking slowly takes on their glow, a light gray tone. I should have known it would be his color— so much about him is black or on the gray scale.

"You're Seelie, aren't you," I state.

He turns from the fading Fae light and smirks. "Yes, but not just any Seelie— the first Seelie. That is a story for another time and place, granddaughter. Sarinah, eat and rest so you may win." He reaches to cup my cheek, and I let him. His eyes soften.

The tender look of paternal love pushes back all his bravado. He blinks and snatches his hand back.

"Any last words of advice before I march off to possible death and dismemberment?" I allow my own bravado to cover my moment of trust. He has risked everything to be here helping me. My neck works to take the tightness away. I've never before felt the love of a grandparent, I had thought they were all dead. But here Puca stands in all his glory— I'm sure he believes he is glorious. Showing me love isn't just a word you say, it's something you do.

"You can only open a portal to a place you've seen. When the end comes, you will need to make a choice. Don't make the obvious one. Chaos or death are simply a stepping stone to something else." Puca locks his jaw down. The wall shimmers behind and pulls apart to reveal the cozy sitting room he took Lavender to. He leaps, and it closes before he lands on the other side. I am alone with all my crazy thoughts.

CHAPTER 20

Deston's words still ring in my head, every action could cost someone I cared about their life. He is blackmailing me by holding them over me. For all I know, he has Zoe, Olive, Brad, and Camille. Though I've got a feeling Brad would rather die than come back.

I could let myself out of this room, I could leave the castle. But what about my friends? What about Arty? What would happen to them? Puca said to stay put.

Wherever Arty is I know he's still alive, and Jacques knows how much he means to me. I showed that hand a long time ago. If I just kept my mouth shut and not been so obsessed about getting both of us out of here, the Fae would never have known.

They took us together. I'm sure Janice told Deston how we were yelling at each other, fighting for each other. They probably thought we were in love. Janice knows better now.

I can stare out the crystal windows till kingdom come, yet it won't change anything.

I have to finish this and quickly.

The door swings silently open, the lock didn't make its usual click. Why bother with the locks when the iron works so much better? But the burning iron magic never wakes out to me from the door. I eye the jam behind my new guest with some interest. What else had they done while I was gone?

Facing my guest, I expected to see Deston, but instead, I am stuck with Pinky, my unwanted, long-lost one-time Fae maid. Her hottie attitude was unchanged. Her lips turn down in a glower.

"Where'd they dig you out of?" I cross my arms and cock a hip out.

"My lady." She narrows her eyes while setting a food tray down. Calling me 'my lady' clearly leaves a sour taste on her tongue.

"What you don't recognize me? Is it the hair or the pointy ears?" I click my tongue.

Her eyes dart over my face and body, brows rising in surprise as she surveys my face.

"No, my lady, I recognize you. Course, you've changed so much since we last saw each other." Pinky's reply is cold and dry and laced with innuendo.

I release a humorless laugh at her discomfort. I don't even remember Pinky's real name. At the time, I didn't care—I was afraid of Fae and wanted to leave. Now I want to stop them, rule them, teach them you can live without being an asshole.

She ran on quickly, trying to hide her feelings. "The rules weren't laid out for everyone. Some of us just thought the princes were toying with humans, creating some distractions to help us all get over our sorrow." Pinky turns her head to inspect the room, searching for something: Lavender maybe? "If I had known, I would've treated you with more respect." The lie wakes off of her. She could've just had it tattooed on her head in day-glo colors, liar. It would look fab in scrolling cursive, with maybe a little tribal line down the side. I smirk at the vision.

"Don't bother with your lies, Pinky. I don't care whether you would've treated me better or not. Leave the tray and go. I have no time, patience, or interest in talking to someone who can't even figure out what the truth is or which side their bread is buttered on," I retort, crossing my arms. Then, thinking twice about it, I loosen them to hang open and ready at my sides.

"Why would you butter bread on both sides?" she inquires with a quirked eyebrow and hitched lips.

"Exactly. You can't answer the question since you don't understand the euphemism. So, you're really just wasting my time. Is there anything else you wanted to say?" I demand.

Her jaw clenches together. I can see it working back and forth as she grinds her teeth, ears wiggling with each clinch.

"You won't rule, you know—they won't allow you to be Queen. No one wants you to be Queen," Pinky spit the venomous words, unable to hold her ire back anymore.

"Just because I'm here and you all hate me, doesn't mean I won't be in charge. And when I am in charge, I'll remember who helped me and who hurt me. You haven't helped." I smile.

I didn't think it was possible for her to become a lighter shade of pink, but she did, Pinky paled.

"My lady, I am UnSeelie, you can never ask us to support a Seelie Queen. We will respect you, follow your orders, but wanting you? That won't happen. We only want our own kind and you cannot fault us for that." It was a plea for understanding.

Her plea fell on the deaf ears of the millions of humans the Fae butchered. In that moment I see how easy it would be to kill all who stood in my way. I tasted this bitterness before with Nikki as I watched her kill Nick. Then again when Jacques used his magical control to force Arty away from me and back to his den of vipers.

"I *can* fault you for it, I don't care if you want your own kind. If it hadn't been for the last Queen this whole charade would never have happened. She's the one who told you to go to the surface, where you'd find the next Queen. She's the one who put all of this into action, and if it wasn't for her and her vindictive nature all those humans would not have had to die." I shift from one foot to the other, keeping my stance open for attack. I don't care what the rules said about challengers. Deston had already sent one assassin, so why not another? "But you guys don't give a shit. You don't care who you hurt or kill. You're too busy running around acting like crazy, wild people with no manners. Apparently, no one's ever taught you."

The vision of Deston's smug smile after he kissed me brings on a desire to gag. The UnSeelie are cancer to be culled from the world. They feel no remorse for all the suffering they brought to the world. The UnSeelie Queen did all this, and they wanted another Queen just like her.

I want to turn my back on her lying Fae face. She's telling the truth about the UnSeelie court. They will never accept or respect me. It'll be a constant battle, and everything I say is going to be twisted and used for some nefarious purpose.

I begin again. "You know, I don't need you to stay and watch me eat. I'm perfectly capable of getting a fork to my own mouth without a babysitter." I throw the words over my shoulder at her. I just want her to leave. Hearing no reply, I turn and steal a glance at her.

Lyra, her name was Lyra. I dredged that one up from the fat file of I don't care.

She crosses her arms, without saying a word and stands her ground, refusing to leave until I'd eaten. I fake calm under her scrutiny— her actions made me suspicious. Nothing about the food gives off a strange wake. It all looks perfectly normal, but it's always perfectly normal until it isn't.

Doesn't matter, tomorrow's the final challenge. I can't run the risk of being weakened by hunger, and the food tastes normal enough. But with the butterflies in my stomach pulling flip-flops I hardly taste any of it. A glass of some kind of juice is off to the side. I've never been much of a juice drinker, instead preferring water and coffee or tea. My mother said juice was poison. The wakes coming off it are normal and it smells flowery and sweet.

"I'm finished, so can you go now? I'd like to go to sleep before I murder or get murdered tomorrow." I give her a pinched tight-lipped smile.

"My instructions were to not leave until you had finished the entire tray." She plasters a half smile on her face and cocked her hip to one side mimicking me.

I curl one side of my face at her. It's a snarl, but I didn't care. Tomorrow I'll either be dead or running this whole shit show. "The tray is empty unless of course, you're blind as well as stupid." I threw the last part in out of spite while wiping my lips on the silky cloth napkin and throwing it on the tray for good measure.

"I beg your pardon, 'my lady,' but you still have something left—a drink, I believe," Lyra gives her smug reply and points at the seemingly innocuous cup.

Now I found her cheeky pressing of the subject not only curious but suspicious. "What's so special about the juice?"

My eyes linger on the cup, but under scrutiny, it comes up boring. The wakes say it is normal, inert.

"There is nothing special about it. I'll prove it." She snatches up the glass, takes the smallest sip in the world. Then, she extends the cup toward me.

I take it in my hand and sniff at its flowery, sticky sweetness, then take a big gulp, setting the remainder down on the tray.

"See? All done. Now go!" I spit at her.

Her face painted with a self-satisfied smile, she picks up the tray and saunters out of the room. She hums the cleaning song as she goes, and the tray cleans itself.

Before the door closes, I know what she did. She took just enough of a sip to get me to drink— it was her job to trick me. They sent Lyra because Lavender was gone. Besides, Lavender wouldn't have done it.

My mother was right, juice is poison—why didn't I listen?

My vision darkens around the edges. My muscles loosen, and I relaxed back onto the bed. My eyes drift closed and darkness swamps me.

CHAPTER 21

On the edge of my consciousness, a cold permeates, seeping deep into my bones. I roll over, only to encounter more cold. My neck aches from the angle of my head. With a dry mouth and crusty tongue, I smack my lips together, running my tongue around the inside. My eyelids scratch with every blink because they are covered in a crust all their own.

I choose a gray blob and focus on it, only to focus on the dark, silvery gray of dead trees surrounding grayish-black rock. The room wakes of death and decay.

A couple more minutes lying on my side allows my drugged sleep to ease away. Stretching my cramped and achy limbs, I hear the creaking of joints.

Is this how Sleeping Beauty felt when she got up after lying in bed for years? *Did they dust her off?*

Propping my torso up on my elbows and pressing down with my hands, I turn my head to get a good look at the room.

It is round and made of old stones and dead trees—they didn't wake back anything that felt living. I can't tell if the floor was actually rock or wood that has been dead so long it is petrified. The windows in the room are no larger than an archer's perch. Otherwise, it is completely empty, suspiciously vacant of stairs or doors nothing. I can't even discern a break in the flooring.

I rub my hands over my eyes. Maybe if I clear a little more of the foggy drug out, I can see a way to escape. But after rubbing for several minutes and getting rid of all the crusty eye boogies, the visage still hasn't changed. I'm still staring at dead trees and crumbling rocks.

I take to my feet, and the whole structure groans, and the floor shifts. Nothing happens, and other than further groaning from the flooring as I step across the room it doesn't seem as though I am in any immediate danger.

The Fae got me in here somehow, and clearly, I didn't fly through a window — they're too narrow. There must be a way out. All the rocks and wood in the walls fit together seamlessly as if the castle was built as they grew the trees around it.

Everything was odd shapes, and there was no symmetrical meeting of edges. Some of the stones are shaped like triangles, some fit like a puzzle piece right around the branch. Others have branches sticking out of the center as if they'd used the trees themselves like rebar. But it is all dead—long dead. There aren't even any dried leaves or remnants of life. The only thing left in the room is dust and cobwebs.

Cobwebs?

My eyes dart up around the rafters I don't see any spiders, but clearly, there must be some here. They clearly left their mark behind. The cobwebs appear old, but age doesn't mean they're unused—could be a part of their web they'd forgotten or not visited recently. What had Lavender said about spiders in Fae? They're bigger than the ones on the surface? A shiver runs over my body, *bigger spiders*. I shake my head, rubbing my arms up and down over my shoulders. Now I know how Indiana Jones felt when it came to snakes.

The floor groans again, and I slide my feet across the surface. I have to get out of here. Think. However they got me in here is clearly still here, all I have to do is figure it out. I just need to systematically check every stone and branch to see exactly how it fits together and if it comes apart. I go to the window with the most cobwebs around it.

I ran my fingers from the floor to the ceiling. I examine every inch I could reach painstakingly. Taking my time, I examine anywhere that even remotely looked like it might be meeting lines for an opening.

It all ends up being nothing more than just more space on the wall filled with sticks and stones. *Who builds like this?* Construction is supposed to have rhyme and reason. Who am I kidding, this is Fae, so there is no rhyme or reason. It's all about amusing themselves.

Oh my God, that's it. I have to look for the part that has rhyme and reason. Everything else will be whimsical, not making any sense. Throw in the rhyme or reason, not because it makes sense, but because they feel as if it's obtuse simply by putting it there.

I have to take the room as a whole, not in its smaller parts. I put my back to the window, and I can hear the wind howling outside. The rustling caused the eaves of the roof to groan.

It strikes me, one of the windows isn't real. It's fake, like a painting or imaginary a trompe l'ocil. And I fell for it. How much time did I waste scouring this place?

The light outside isn't fading but that no guarantee they didn't enchant the windows so I never know what time it is.

The window I stood beside gives off a cool breeze raising the hairs on my arms. I thrust my arm out to be sure it's real, then pull my arm back in and move to the next one. It has cobwebs lingering around the edges. I rub my hand up and down on my leather britches. The idea of the creepy crawly spider silk clinging to my skin makes every part of me tingle with revulsion. I open and close my eyes a few times, and I thrust my hand into the windows opening, nothing out there but the fading light of Fae illuminating the skin on my arms. The window reveals nothing more than my own day-glo Fae markings. I light up like a Christmas tree. I will never get used to that, I don't care if I live to be a thousand years old. Seeing my own skin light up like a night-light is going to creep me out to the day I died.

I proceed to the final window. I should've seen it before, but I missed it, too busy thinking it was real and not seeing it for what it was—just a trick of Fae: something to make you believe it is something it isn't.

My arm doesn't go through, stopping dead as my fingers crush into a stone hole. I grope around only to stumble upon a wooden lever. I clasp it and pull it down, only to encounter a skittering and click, clicking. Like knitting needles clacking together. It comes closer and grows slowly until finally, it stops. I crank the handle over and the stones swing open to reveal a narrow, winding staircase twisting down into the gloom. I have just enough time to look behind me and see the giant, black, multi-faceted eyes of a spider.

My heart rate shoots through the roof. It came through the thatching and I watch in horror as the last bit of straw falls back into place. The clacking is the spinnerets sticking out of its ass, and it isn't alone, it came with friends.

All three of them are black, with a red star on their bulbous backside. I frequently have nightmares about tarantulas and cane spiders. They were large but compared to these big boys they were nothing more than gag gifts to fool your friends.

These were the mother-of-all Black Widows all lined up on me. I dart my eyes down to the gloomy stairs and seize the rope handle. I whistle up my rope charm and grab ahold, allowing it to drag me down to wherever it led.

My heart beats 1000 times a minute, and the clacking follows after me keeping time with my movements. I chance a glance back to catch they aren't far behind, each one hanging from its own silk cord.

My terror is now palpable, my hands moist with fear. Before I can stop myself, I fall through the break in the rope and tumble to the floor. It only takes a fraction of a second before one pounces on me. Six of its legs lock me in place, pulling me toward its spinners. I crane my head to see the shiny black needles rubbing against each other, oozing the sticky silk from its body. The clacking roars into overdrive, creating more of a vibration versus and old lady knitting in a rocking chair.

I grab a hold of the lip in a step to pull myself away. Anything to get away from this giant bloodsucker. But its legs have some kind of hairy knives locked into my skin. I kick at what I assumed is its thorax, and the adrenaline pulsing through my veins throws my energy into overdrive. The spider rears back, and I whistle at the other half of the rope. The end glistens with its enchantment, waiting for me. I pull my arm free of the little needle-like knives on the spider's foot, but it drags me back at the last second. I scream with frustration and kick out again, using the force of my feet against its belly to leverage myself onto the rope. My hand touches it and I'm pulled away, but the clacking doesn't stop, it simply slows down. One is behind me and one of my feet is covered in spider silk, but where are the others?

The magic tugs on my arm, drawing me down, and my leg is pulled up, dragging me back up. The spider closest to me digs one of his knife-like hairs into the leather of my pants and strains back. A second leg digs into my leg, cutting the leather away. I watch as a mushroom form on a stair, then the wall.

Kicking my foot out, I hum at the silk, hoping to break it, but to no avail.

I've always been told spider silk was one of the strongest fibers on the planet. That, pound for pound, it is stronger than steel. This was mega-mondo silk. *I'm so fucked.* The pulling and yanking causes my ankle to pop any moment it will dislocate and I'll be really screwed. With my free hand I pull a finger blade from my bodice and toss it up the stairs, then sing a bit from a James Bond movie, Tom Jones was always one of my favorites. I picture the knife slicing the silk threat. To my delight it does and I snap free in an instant, reaching the bottom of the stairs. An arched with a door nestled in it, without another thought I'm through and forcing it shut.

No sooner did I begin the locking song and the door pushes open. Screaming, I put another burst of energy into the shove, already in motion. One of the appendages pierces the heavy door. I pull another knife and stab it. A cutting scream comes through from the other side and it rears back. I slam it shut and sing the lock home only taking a breath when I hear the click.

I turn and lean my head against the heavy wooden door. Whistling a protection seal over the opening, I bent over to catch my breath and survey my surroundings.

I'm awake, now where the fuck am I?

The hallway goes one direction, so I head down the dimly lit corridor, embracing the shadows lining the walls. Cobwebs line the hallway and linger in the archways. Some doors still hang in their frames, and others lay on their side. A few are angled away from what was once their home. All carry the silvery white of long-dead wood weathered by sun and sea.

Much of the structure is cracked or split. Dust trickles down from the upper beams. I'm unable to discern whether an upper floor exists, or the dust is caused by nothing more than my passage disturbing the air.

A high creak cuts the otherwise dead calm, followed by a click.

I freeze in place and hum a shadow around me while pressing my back to the wall.

I spy movement— a shadow flickers back and forth as a girl passes through the dim Fae light. Her white hair reflects the day-glo colors as rainbows shoot over the dingy surfaces.

I turn and glance over my shoulder, the hallway ends at my tower door. There's no way I'm going back that direction.

The girl turns the only corner off the long avenue. I watch the wake waves; other than her passing all is quiet on the western front.

Tiptoeing down the hallway, I follow the shadows, leaving no dust trail behind. *I might have to kill her.* I don't want to kill, but this is a kill-or-be-killed scenario. Who am I kidding, this place is filled with predators. I can't be the only one? I am a predator, I've killed. I clench my teeth, pressing my lips flat. Whatever I do, it's for everyone.

Even as I let the justification fill my mind, I am not sure it's right. I reach back and scratch at the bulge on my back. My nerves make it vibrate with movement.

The corner looms in my vision and I press my body flat to the wall as I inch up to the edge. The groan of dry old wood breaks the silence of my cat-and-mouse game. I wait for the patter of footsteps to drift away before I make a move.

I dart a glance around the corner, and lingering in a doorway poised and ready to strike stands a vapid willowy, Fae-looking Camille.

I press my head back against the wall and stare up at the ceiling. *Why did it have to be Camille? Why can't be any other sort of human girl?*

If I enchant her, maybe I can slip by and be done with it. My whistle of enchantment fills the air, only to be cut off by dry laughing.

Camille calls out, "Whoever you are I'm too Fae for that to work anymore. Show me who you are and let's get this over with." She steps out from the shadowy doorway, standing between me and my objective.

In her taunting, oh-so-familiar voice, Camille continues, "Are you scared? Worried you can't take me? I'm as well-trained as the next contender, you might have a chance. After all, aren't we all human?" She smiles.

A high-pitched sound whizzes past my face, followed by a loud thump. A bolt from a crossbow lodges itself in the wall next to my head.

"Awe, I almost hit you. You look familiar, do I know you?" Camille inquires.

Leaping to my full height, I charge her.

"I guess this is a fight I've been expecting," I say.

A smile sneers half her face. "Oh yeah, I've been waiting for this. Little miss perfect, are you ready to meet your maker, Sarah? I've been wanting to kick your ass for years." She sprints, launching both feet at me and collides with my chest, forcing all the air from my lungs.

Recoiling from the impact, I slam into the far wall. My head makes a sickening smack on the stone, then I slide to the floor and stare up at Camille's shadowed face.

"Statistically I'm due for a win, and I feel lucky." Her lips pull back in a macabre smile. I haul my arm over my torso just before she stomps a foot down on top of it. She tugs a knife from a sheath on her bodice and smiles at the metallic twang it makes. Then, flexing her shoulders, she raises her arm to strike.

"Do you want to know what happened to Brad?" I sputter.

Her arm freezes its downward thrust.

I'm buying time to make the stars go away, blinking to push the mist back.

"Brad's dead, I killed him in the enchanted bubble," Camille says and falters, and her lip trembles before she presses them together into a thin line.

I rush into the gap, trying to keep her thinking and off guard. "Brad isn't dead, I took him back to the surface myself. Before the enchanted bubble. The bubble wasn't real." My words work their way around inside my head. She saw Brad and killed him, but he wasn't there. What did that mean for Nick? I shove that out of my mind. *I don't have time for that.*

I press myself up off the floor to face her. "Nicely played, Sarah, using my emotions against me. Brad's dead. He attacked me and I killed him. I didn't want to, but it was him or me." She releases a crazed snicker. Her eyes are filled with wild hysteria as the color changes, shifting from one to another.

I need to get away from crazy Camille.

Her arm cuts down in a flash. I catch her hand, holding the tip of the blade inches away from my breastbone.

"Die, like all the rest, just die." Her other hand curls around the pommel of the hilt. Her eyes are wide and wild as the muscles in her neck and shoulders strain against my continued resistance. Taking a light breath so as not to telegraph my next move, I pull a dagger from my bodice and stab it into her side.

Camille cries out, "You dirty bitch!" Tears fill her eyes as her free hand pulls the blade from her torso with a sick sucking sound.

With both hands, I push the dagger pointed at my chest off course and release my grip. It digs into a seam between two stones and lodges itself there. But her body keeps going. I slip away from her, only to watch in horror as she slams into the small dagger still held in her hand. The blade pierces her skin, burying itself deep in her belly.

An agonizing scream cut the hallway in half and Camille slides down the stone wall, leaving a bloody trail behind before she lands face first on the floor.

With a horror-filled realization, I scamper back to her side— my numb fingers work to turn her over.

She coughs, and blood-filled spittle edges her lips. "Why can't I win?" she mutters.

Blood pours from the gash in her belly. My finger dagger is nowhere to be seen. I press my hand over the opening. Camille coughs again and her innards threaten to slip between my fingers like wet ropes. Closing my eyes, I swallow back the saliva pooling in my mouth.

This isn't what I want. I thought Camille and I would go off to college and see each other at school reunions or on Twitter feeds. I don't want her dead, not really.

Opening my eyes, I survey the slowing rise and fall of her chest. "Camille." I shake her. "Look at me! I can't heal you unless you let me. Sing with me."

Her eyes slowly focus on me. "You can't heal me, you have to love me for that. A Fae told me so. You hate me." Her eyes roll around and back into her head. I can't say I love her—I don't. We fought our entire childhood. Always exchanging verbal blows. Until today, though, we had never hit each other.

Janice said you had to care. I cared, I did. I hope it's enough. "I do care, Camille, so help me."

Her eyes blink, refocusing on me. "I wish this had never happened. I'd still be with Brad." She whispers her desire as the tears run down the sides of her cheeks, creating dust-free streams. "I love Brad, but I never told him. He put up with all my crap, and I don't know why. Then I killed him, I didn't want to." Blood escapes the side of her lips to run down to her neck and into the once-blond-but-now-white Fae hair.

Leaning over, I kiss her forehead.

At least she'd been loved. Brad loved her, I know he did. I watched the way Brad's eyes followed her as if there was only one sun and it shone with her. I'd been jealous of it.

My eyes burn with tears I can never shed. I pet Camille's hair back from her forehead, wiping away the remands of my bloody kiss. *I can do this.*

The rumble begins in my chest, spreading out and surrounding Camille. In the background, Camille hums sad and broken notes. But my magic overwhelms hers and we join, creating a common bond that wakes over her. I watch as it dives in, swirling like a mixing bowl to rearrange the broken and repair the damage.

The first cry rips from Camille, then another. Her body withers in pain, twisting one way then the other.

Pulling air in through my nose, I push it out on a song through my mouth. My eyes train on her stomach. One side of my dagger's handle peeks out of her flesh. The magic wakes eject the foreign object.

As soon as the handle is free, I yank it free of her flesh. My singing reaches a crescendo. The wound knits the gash closed. Camille cries, clawing at me, each note reaching a new pain level. I find new heights on each verse until I'm certain she is completely healed. I watch in fascination, her hair changes from white to dark blond. Her face rounds out with those human features I grew up with.

I allow the magic to drift away on ever-diminishing wake waves. Camille stops moving. Feeling for a pulse, I find one— slow and steady.

Wiping my hands on her shirt, I stand up. The hall holds several doors, so I move to the closest and yank it open. The dust on the floor is undisturbed, and no cobwebs line the corners or windows.

Whistling Camille into a floating lump, I pull her inert form into the room and move her to a side wall.

I hum the rotting tapestries hanging by the window down from their wooden rings. I drag one over and ball it under her head, and the other I lay over her body.

Camille's eyes flutter open. "Sarah, I'm hungry." She mutters.

I laugh.

"Yeah, I was too after I was healed. Takes a lot out of you. Listen, you need to stay here quietly." She smacks her lips, and I whistle up some water in my hand and give her a sip.

I push her hair back from her forehead, revealing a rounded, human-looking ear.

"You look different, I can't see the magic anymore. Does this mean I can go home?"

I shake my head. "I don't know. But if you lay here a while I'll try to send you home."

She smiles, and her eyes drift shut. I step back and sing the enchanting song, locking her into a lost bubble of time; she won't age or die until someone finds her. Then lean out of the doorway, and whistle the rocky rubble littering the hall up into the air and move them into the room, keeping my eyes off the pool of blood on the floor.

Camille resembles Snow White lying in wait for her prince. I gather the dusty rubble into a pasty puddle on the floor and begin stacking stones.

My intent is to wall her in. If they don't know she's here, they won't bother her. Taking one last look at her sleeping face, I lodged the last stone in place. Within minutes I have closed her off from the world.

Stopping only for a moment at the door, I look back. If I don't win, she'll lie there for all time. Taking a deep breath, I leave the room. *All the more reason to end this. As if I don't have enough to carry around.*

I turn the corner of the hall, only to find more hallways leading off into a distant unknown. Once again I pick my way around, searching my surrounding for wake waves that didn't belong.

I meet only ordinary stones and long-forgotten castle rot.

Arched doorways lead to multitudes of rooms in varying states of decay. Finally, I come to a stairwell. Twisting down into the shadowy depths, I follow the turning until it come to an end.

The archer windows are my only clue to the outside world, but my eyes only meet more air with more towers off in distance. I press my face to the side in an attempt to gauge height. Other than a best guess, I could be ten stories or forty, I can't tell. The ground is still a long way off.

CHAPTER 23

The stairs take me to a new passageway extending to nowhere.

Lovely.

The walls lining the hallway lay on their sides as if a child had knocked them all down in a haphazard fashion. I move around what I can and climb over several. The groaning of the structure meets my every step. The stone weakly wake back to me, warning of their impending failure.

My senses scream to get out of here. But there is nowhere to go except straight ahead. I trudge on, floating over any area where wakes hardly register. The scent of dust and mold lingers in the air.

Fae always smells of flowers, a thick drugging perfume of it. The air here is gritty. Cupping my hand, I hum water into it and quickly gulp it away. I rub the leftover moisture from my hand on the sleeve of my shirt.

The room shifts and I stumble to the left. Rubble shifts around me and the sound of tumbling rocks is followed by a crunching footfall.

The sound of lips smacking together is my first warning. A long sucking snort is followed by a throat clearing hack and a deep breath. The spit is hurled against the wall two feet from where I am concealed by fallen debris. I watch the green globby mess slide down the stony edifice.

A grunt followed by a juicy fart completes the picture of nasty.

"Is that end clear? We can't miss one. This may be our last chance." A raspy voice inquires.

"No, I haven't checked the stairs, but I need a piss first. Don't worry, if we get them all, wild gets to continue ruling and so do we." The reply comes out wet with smacking lips. A steaming stream of urine spouts from above, arching over the rockpile to splatter on the floor a few inches from my shoes. Little drops splash back, landing on my boots and leggings. The heavy scent of ammonia and copper fills the air.

I cover my mouth to keep from gagging, pulling my magical shadow cloak tighter with a light rumble from my throat.

"Did you hear that?" smacking lips inquires.

"No. Now finish up, we need to move closer to the ground. Wild will get them if we don't," Thirsty retorts.

I listen to the rock-crushing footsteps retreating, following every groan of the building.

I hope it doesn't fall down while I'm crouching next to the piss puddle.

Silence rules once again, and I move from my hiding place. I pick my way over the rocks along the wall. The rubble hides their footprints. I came to a T, but neither hall looks any safer than the other. The walls wake back a disturbance to the left while the right is dead as a doornail.

Left it is.

They said they needed to reach the ground floor. I probably don't have a drop of human left in me. The Fae side has taken over raising my senses. Now, when hair rose on the back of my neck, I don't shake it away. A rock rolls behind me, and I dart a glance back. A magic wake follows a line through an arched doorway as if someone darted out of sight. *I'm being followed, great.*

I press against the wall as flat as paper. Inching down the wall, I see a large pile of debris covering the hall from wall to wall. Something red bobs in and out of sight just on the other side.

Off in the distance, a scream breaks the silent peace, then another more terrified than the first. A huffing laugh followed by smacking lips wakes into my back.

My heart picks up speed to race faster with every breath, making me whip my head one way then the other. I can't go back, and forward is the screaming.

I moisten my lips and whistle rocks into the air. At the same time, I hurl them behind me and make a mad dash to the rubble. I crest the top in time to catch a glimpse of a small goblin-like creature wearing a dripping red hat and thick leather boots. He carries a large meat cleaver in one hand and scratches his exposed plumber's crack with the other.

The floor groans and shifts, straining with the change in weight and movement. One moment it is groaning, and the next I watch in horror as a giant section of the floor falls, leaving behind a gaping hole. Dust plumes press into every corner, blocking my vision. Another creaking groan comes along with a crashing of stones, and my firm footing turns into the world tilting at a 45-degree angle. I never knew you could surf with stone, but the narrow stone I was standing on slides down onto the next floor. All I can do is keep my balance and footing. Rocks and pebbles pelt me from behind. My stone surfboard becomes a tilt-a-whirl, and I slip off and slam into edge of the gaping crevasse teetering there before sliding down to the next level.

Instinctively, I cradle my arms around my head, protecting my newly healed face. A hollow boom followed by a screaming squeak of wood pulling apart tears the air. The choking dust finds its way into my nose and mouth, coating my tongue with grit. Running my tongue around the inside of my mouth to gather saliva, I spit the gritty chunks of rubble away. The floor shifts again, and I shift with it on to my back. My head cracks against the cold unforgiving stone.

I blink back the stars in my eyes, then feel for the tender spot on the back of my skull. My fingers probe, but came back dry—there would be no tell-tale mushrooms to mark my presences.

The sound of smacking lips slips past me under the dusty cover.

"Call out, brothers, there was one still up there before the floor fell." His lips smack with moisture on every word.

How is he not coughing?

A voice calls down from above. "Gral, there's no one left up here. She must be down there." A few pebbles fall on my head.

"We have fresh kills, so don't waste your time looking for the straggler, Tarnnel. We know where she's going." The gravelly voice from earlier drifts up to me. I pull the shadowy magic closer around me. Tarnnel must be the lip smacker. The dust gives me cover, but lack of visibility heightens sound.

A humph from a hard landing off to the left reminds me, it's time to move. I time my steps with that of the goblin, anticipating our distance and keeping it.

"Ween, call the wind to clear this dust, I can't see the blood," Tarnnel calls to a third. I freeze in place. The scent of rotting meat and congealed blood wafts over from the dwarf-like creature.

If I open my mouth to breathe, I take in dust; if I keep breathing through my nose, I'll retch. I pull the front of my chemise up over my nose. My own scent of dirt and sweat is preferable to a meat market without power for a week.

My goblin cover was on the move again, and I match his steps, moving down to the next floor. My footing finds a level surface and a breeze filters through the outline of an arched door. I move closer to the opening, hoping to follow a wall and keep to the safety of the shadows.

The light breeze turns to a blowing gale, clearing the hallway in under two minutes. I find myself standing a few feet from a wall and surrounded by no less than five stunted little goblins with dripping-wet red hats.

"I told you she was down here," Ween quips. He pulls a large meat cleaver from over his shoulder. He lips pull back into a leering smile, revealing a mouth filled with pointed blood-stained teeth. The cleaver's edge gleams with an eerie light and rust-colored stains. The blade itself is a rectangle with a curling hook on the top edge next to a hole. He heaves it up and down, allowing the back of the blade to smack into his meaty paws.

"She smells different from the others, Gral." Trennal smacks his lips and wipes his dripping nose across his sleeve. The wet trail from his nose began its course anew from his nose down to his lips. The mucus from his nose was making his lips wet.

I screwed up my nose on one side, *gross.*

Trennal pulls two blades from either side of his stunted torso. The blades resemble his friend's, encrusted with rust.

Gral's gravelly voice cuts through the tension. "I can't smell her over the others. Make short work of her and let's go. I don't want to miss out on the rest." He reaches up and scratches at the red-pointed stocking cap stuck to his head, then pushes the brim back, leaving a red gleaming trail behind. I watch in morbid fascination as the red trail coalesces and runs down the side of his gnarled face to drip off the wispy hair on his jawline.

The fear I should feel from their words didn't hit full force until I scan the rest of the hall. Three girls lay in different positions, all with unseeing eyes staring into a future they would never reach. Two with white hair and one with black, all had blood as red as a cherry. Next to each one stoops a hatless goblin. Their bald heads shined with rosy moisture. One hand held on to a cap as they used them to wipe up the bloody pool surrounding each girl.

"Gral, can this one be mine? I want her." Trennal smacks his lips and pulls them back into a smile of glee. *Oh, I'm fucked.* The sound of three wet hats slapping onto the bald pates of the goblins made me swallow back the saliva pooling in my mouth.

I refocus on the leader and Trennal.

Gral replies, "Finish it quick, we won't wait!"

The four turn to follow the hallway to the next stairwell. In the flash of an instant, I'm on my back, blinking back the stars again. Trennal's beady black orbs stare down at me emotionlessly as he studies me. He flips one of the knives in his hand, turning it over, the blade pointed down and away from him.

I kick a leg up at him and it meets his hip, knocking him off balance. Then, I let my magic rumble begin. I turn to my old standby, lifting rocks and dust and spinning my magic tornado.

The flying debris pelts his body. But he is up like lightning and moves into the maelstrom.

"I'm not worried about a little dirty wind, human," Trennal taunts.

I don't take the bait. Instead, I put one of Puca's lessons to good use. I picture myself at the other end of the corridor and appear there.

"You're a tricky one, I'll give you that." Trennal remarks. "You'll have to be smarter than that to beat me. We Redcaps live a long time. It's the blood, it gives us immortality. Your blood should last me a century at least." He sucks in a long, wet snuffle and runs his sleeve under his nose. It does nothing to slow the flow of mucus from his nasal passage.

Using my power to move in an instant, I hopscotch down the stairs to the next floor. Smacking lips keeps pace behind me with each new flash. I am never going to shake him this way.

Bursting from the curved stairwell, I have enough time to scan the corridor before I flash to the other end.

Magic wakes turn to the left at the end of the passageway and continue on. I scramble over a new pile of debris for my next flash and come face to face with a gnarled visage. One side of his face is scrunched up as if squished by giant fingers. His black marble eye blinks twice.

The shock of our meeting wears off, and he raises his cleaver over his head. I flash a kick to his exposed gut, knocking him down the other side of the rubble.

"She's over here, Trennal, come kill her before we do," Gral calls.

Taking in the new terrain, I'm surrounded by five little goblin-like creatures, their redcaps dripping with blood the scent of rotten meat lingers along with the dust.

The goblin with the pinched face jumps to his feet takes a breath and flashes to my side. I have enough time to face him, then I hang in the air for a split second and the floor drops out and gravity takes over. Humming, I create a floating spell. Pinch face tumbles down to the next floor, only to be covered by rocks and wooden beams.

I float down light as a feather. The crashing of stone on stone covers Pinch face's head, followed by a sickening crunch. His hat changes from red to an earthy brown then shrivels down to the size of a garden gnome.

Glancing up through the gaping hole above me, I can finally see them for what they are. Nothing more than garden gnomes with redcaps. *Who the fuck ever thought these were cute?*

Crunching rock reverberates off what's left of the walls. A moment later I land flat on my back next to the open lifeless staring eyes and a pool of blood. I return the fixed stare with one of surprises. Dripping followed by slapping fills the dust-laden air, and behind me, a sickening squish filters through the grimy air. Scrambling to my feet, I spy other bodies littering what's left of both upper and lower hallways. None of the blood grew mushrooms. The dead girls are still too human. I cough on dust and grim, to cover the cry clawing to get out.

The rumble starts in my chest moving outward to fill the space around me lifting every object into a floating position.

Smacking followed by a fart causes me to turn and duck as Trennal slashes his cleaver at my head. He misses most of me, but rends a hole in my shirt, nicking my arm. The blue blood wells up and drips onto the floor.

A deep blue mushroom sprouts, glowing with internal Fae light throwing its gloom over the already creepy scene.

Whistling up the wind, I push all the floating gnomes out of my way. "Don't bother, brothers, she's too Fae—her blood's no good to us," Trennal yells as he spins away in the windy vacuum.

Gral replies, "But if we kill her the rule of wild continues."

A blade whizzes past my face and I hum it into my hand, then return it to its owner only to miss. Multiple thumps are followed by crunching and a grunt.

Using the wind to clear the dust, I can't win without visibility.

"Wenn, fix her Fae tricks!" Gral demands.

Wenn follows with, "it's raining, it's pouring, the old man is snoring. He went to bed and bonked his head and the Fae took him before the morning." Wenn's voice rings out the counter to my magic. My eyes find the source of four grunts as each gnome finds his feet.

I hum my protection around me along with my shadowy cloak, then flash to the other end of the passage. The yawning archway promises an exit to a new floor.

And I flash down the twisting tower at breakneck speed. But the gnomes keep pace, flashing past five floors and down two corridors before coming to a large room edged on all four sides with balconies only to meet on the far side into one open stairway. It trails down one floor, then splits back into two. I count at least ten levels, the lower the floor the darker the gaping abyss.

Whipping, my head back and forth like any normal prey, I flash to the top of the second flight. I rumble in the shadows, pulling away the light.

The first gnome turns the corner, following the balcony's edge. I pull a finger blade and throw it and watch the magic wake pushing it to maximum speed. It buries in Gral's chest, and then I thrust it deep into the cavity, slicing through the gnarled heart hidden there.

Flashing to his side, I watch as he sinks down to his knees, clasping at the bloody hole in his sternum. His redcap slips over the edge into the black chasm, desiccating and shriveling as it goes till it carries no more weight than a feather drifting from one side to the other.

One down, three to go.

The knotted, ugly face transforms before me. What had appeared to be a gnarled gnome or goblin fades away to reveal its true form. A young human boy no more than seven. The magic of the cap had twisted him into that horrible beast. I scream in frustration. Everything in Fae is fucked. Evil is good, good is evil.

Why can't just one creature I kill be bad, for real?

I pound my fist into the wall, it crumbles as the plaster falls away. I swallow back my rage and flash back to the lower levels.

CHAPTER 24

The shadows cloak me, and I pull back into their inky embrace. Fae sight works best at night, but even mine can't discern gnome from shadow. My only saving grace is the wake waves. They tattle on everyone, lighting each object similar to dolphin sonar.

The three remaining redcaps breach the archway and come to a halt. The fallen form of Gral is on full display before them. They each take a different direction.

I flash to the next floor down, buying time for my next move, enchanting as I go. I'm banking on them flashing down the stairs and only touching down in a few locations. I hum several protection circles, hoping to trap one or two.

Wenn is their caster, the only one with magic.

"We know you're out there, Fae," Trennal taunts me as he flashes down another level.

They murmur amongst themselves, and each heads a different direction at every floor. I flash down to the next landing while humming the next trap. Then, I step into the shadows, cloaking my movements. I am ready to flash to the next floor, but a redcap appears in one of my circles. He clasps his sickle-shaped weapon in both hands. A smile scrapes across his withered face, sinking his eyes into deep crevasses and forcing the warts to stand out.

"I got her! Next floor, brothers," Wart boy yells to his creepy friends. Ternnal flashes next to him. I flash to the balcony on the other side of the room just outside my next trap. The wakes from the other side ticks back from the protection circle as it takes hold.

"Wenn, I can't move—save me!" Warty screams in irritation. The edge of his sickle scrapes over the magical barrier. Wenn's song fills the air while working over the trap, to no avail. I sang it fresh into the world of magic—the old counter song would never break what I brought forth.

I hitch a half smile and flash to the next floor down.

The gravelly voices three floors up reverberate back and forth, throwing angry wakes in every direction.

"Sorry, Bagga, but I can't get ya out." Wenn's statement only fortifies my belief that my magic is stronger than theirs.

Bagga's screams cut the air; they must have left him behind. I flash down to the next floor, deeper into the chasm. I've lost count how many flights I passed—there must be a bottom. But every flash brings the fear they'd dug a stairwell deep enough to reach China.

The light at the end of this hole is rectangular. I flash to the center, landing at the base of a window. The glass is colored with the stained pieces of crystal, each shaped to fill a part of a picture. Dirt and age mask the visage, leaving only the outline of a woman standing next to what appears to be a stag. The horns rise even higher than the woman's head, and I can only just make out the cloven hooves in the glass closest to me. I crane my next back to get a better view, but only a dim light filters through. I can't make out the color of the woman's hair—it could have been white, but the age and filth clinging to the crystal obscure all but a raised outline.

Dust and gravel filter down and land on my head and shoulders. I lay my trap encompassing the entire landing, then flash to the upper balcony to watch and wait.

Stepping back into the shadows, I pull the gloom of them around me.

Wenn flashes first onto a stair above the landing. He turns his head, surveying the area, taking a moment to examine the window. I hold my breath as his leg breaks the magic barrier and he plants both feet on the landing. He moves cautiously into the center. "Trennal, it's clear!" Wenn calls out.

Trennal flashes onto the opposite rise and waits for a few moments, then raises his foot in the air, only to place it back down. He grabs the handrail and leaps over the side and onto the next flight down.

Fuck, I bit my lip. One to go.

Wenn moves to join him and smashes against the invisible wake line holding him. He opens his mouth to sing, but the sound bounces against the wakes and returns to batter him.

Following the wall and the shadows, I move along the balcony directly across from the window and the stairs. The Fae light glints through the crystal, highlighting the image for a second—I see wings, then it's gone. I shake my head to remove the spots; I've grown so accustomed to the dark. I'm still blinking when my face smashes into the banister, then splintering wood and the weightlessness of freefall replace my vision.

I float before gravity takes over, and the wind pulls at me as the ground rapidly approached. I hum, but the impact pushes the air from my lungs. As panic overwhelms my senses, I struggle to force air into my chest. It rattles and then the rumble ignites, creating my own skin of protection.

"I told you I'd get you," Ternnal's lips smack out. The heavy thump of Ternnal landing next to my battered body is followed by a long snort.

I move to stand, but a blood-covered boot presses into the side of my head, forcing my face into the grimy floor. I blink away the grit, blowing away dust bunnies with my nostrils. The weight of his boot grows, coupled with a long bout of flatulence.

Ternnal calmly orders, "Release Wenn and Bagga!" He snorts phlegm into the back of his throat and hocks it on to the ground not far from my face.

I cough out a dry laugh. "You think I'll free your friends to help kill me? You have the brain of a six-year-old." Internally, I cross my fingers I got his real age correct.

Ternnal's blade slides into my line of sight and taps the stone a whisker away from my nose. Smacking his lips together, he draws in a deep breath. "Fae like pretty. Wouldn't it be a shame to ruin your pretty?" His remark would have scared the shit out of me just a few months ago, but not now.

Pretty and ugly are nothing more than a state of mind—the outside can be altered. Love is the only thing able to create beauty.

I'm buying time to regain my strength. The small area of the room within my line of sight sits empty and littered with chipped stones, splintered wooden timbers, and dust.

I blink away the settling particles and the shadows beyond shift. Ternnal lifts the blade and announces. "Say goodbye to your nose, little Fae." His boot rocks my head back and forth against the stone.

I move my body in time with him, working my hand over a blade handle. With his last rock, I roll away and fling the blade, slicing his swing arm.

I pull my legs up toward my face and back to the ground, I use the momentum to launch onto the balls of my feet. Sliver slides from its scabbard with a chilling ring and melds to my hand. I flash to the base of the stairs.

Ternnal roars, "You can't get away, stupid Fae-ling." He flashes to my side and attacks with his cleaver, cutting left then right.

I parry both attempts to cleave me in two, and the metal rings like sweet bells on Christmas Day. Moving up the stairs, I lure him on. He continues the attack, slashing and thrusting. I fend off, bobbing this way and that taking a new step back each time.

"You Fae-lings always retreat, but at least you put up a fight. Unlike humans." He spits a loogie at me, as he says it. "Humans are worthless," Ternnal snarls on the last word.

"That's funny… aren't you human? I mean, without that disgusting hat you're just like them," I respond with shallow breaths and a raging heart. One more step.

"I haven't been human in thousands of years. My cap made me more." His reply lights up his eyes and he raises the heavy cleaver over his head.

Waiting for the last possible moment, Ternnal leans in, pushing his full strength behind the blow. I step to the side turning at the same time and plant my foot in his ass as he passes by, adding a whistle for extra force.

Ternnal trips over the final tread and tumbles into the protection bubble. His cap slips off his head and lands next to me.

"No! Give me my cap back, I'll do anything you want. I don't need to kill you. I'll make the others stop, I promise." Ternnal crawls on his knees, hands clasped in front of him.

"Swear fealty to me for all time." My eyes dart from Trennal to Wenn. "You, too, Wenn, or I'll leave you in there to die." I snarl.

Both gnomes' mouths open and close like guppies. Ternnal sputters, "Yes, I swear to serve you for all time. You are my lady, I will obey you in all things." He lowers his head and sniffles.

I shift my attention to Wenn. "What about you? You want to die in there?"

Wenn replies, "I'll never die with this cap." He lifts his chin in defiance and scratches his hip.

"Have it your way. Forever is a long time by yourself." I hum and the cap at my feet bursts into flames. The scent of cooking blood permeates the stairwell.

Trannel cries out, "No, no I'll die. The Queen told me! I was given a choice: wear the cap or die." He slumps down on his belly and stares at the charred cinders and ash that once held his redcap of enchantment.

I watch the enchantment fade. The gnarled edges of his face smooth into baby plump cheeks with a rosy hue. His eyes turn from hard black obsidian to blue and he grows three inches. The last change is his nose—it stops running.

Tears clog his eyes, and the little boy before me curls into a little ball, both arms wrapped around his knees. He buries his head into the crevasse where his knees met.

"Maw, where's me Maw?" Ternnal calls out in thickly accented English.

My heart twists for him. "Ternnal, what year is it?" I inquire while turning to survey the cavernous room.

"I know not." He sniffles, as his nose starts to run again.

He is too young to remember, and his wording strikes me as strange. How long had he been wearing that hat?

Wenn pulls his cap down over his ears and moves to the far side of the bubble. "Ya won't be takin my cap, no way no how. I've lived a long time and I intend to keep livin. I don't want to be a crumpled-up fool snivlin for me Maw," he announces.

"Have it your way. When I win I'll be back to kill you. You have till then to decide." I hum a protection line in the bubble to keep Ternnal safe from Wenn. I can't risk Wenn killing him for his blood. "Which way to the throne room?" I demand. Wenn huffs and sits down with his back to me.

The little shit. I turn to survey my surroundings, and what magic lingers in the air. The only vibrations come from above—challengers. I flash under a balcony ledge to hide my presence.

The walls are lined with arches, at least fifty of them. I spy stairs, some leading up, others down. My gut tells me no more stairs. Every other arch goes straight ahead. None give any indication of direction.

Light flashes through the stained glass again, illuminating the outer edges. There is a color pattern, brown-green-blue. It repeats on both sides and the bottom. The top is blank. It makes sense the top represented the stairs with no arches. The sides and bottom of the window represent the walls lining the room. The stairs that are browns go down, blues ones go up, greens go straight.

I call the wind and push some of the dust from the glass. My eyes search every square inch, till I land on the odd man out: a gold piece in a sea of none.

I turn my back to the window to get my bearings. And count down the right side. I check over my shoulder to make sure I had it right. Number eight is my golden ticket, and I take it.

Moving with determination, I cross the room and head down the corridor, biting my lip as I go.

CHAPTER 25

The hall travels on straight into more gloom with no exit that I can discern. I come to the first of many archways and peered in for a quick peek before moving on.

Most rooms have chairs, or tables, desks and books in varying degrees of decay. One resembles a library. *Note to self: check this out later.* Telling myself that is the only way to pull myself away. The information stored there is as drugging as the juice I was given before bed.

I pick up my pace down the passage—there's no need to waste time. The hall ends in a large room.

Voices rip around me laughing like the tinkling of bells. A gagging stench of rotten eggs permeates the air. I can hear them, but I can't see them. I wish I had my bandana to cover the smell. The sound—high, sweet and playful—whips by me. This isn't a normal room. Why, oh why, hadn't I paid more attention? Every area of this castle is laced with ghosts and scary creatures. *I could have picked any passage, but no I had to gamble on a stained-glass window.*

A high arched ceiling disappears into the deep shadows, and the walls echo my steps back at me. Small banquette-style alcoves line the walls on both sides. Threadbare, multicolored cushions wiggle with pink young still sleeping inside their clever nest. The fabric color faded away long ago, leaving only hints of greens, pinks, yellows, and blues, reminding me of a rococo design or something left over from a French king. Rotting drapes, sag from wooden rings, blocking my view into various alcoves.

Trouble lurks on the other side, and I shiver with a with cold certainty.

Giggling and murmuring whip past me and a line of blood forms across my arm as if I was sliced by a knife. Even in the Fae light, it looks dark blue. I rub it off with my sleeve.

"Sarah, Sarah," The many voices whisper my name in every direction using a teasing, singsong voice, goading me. I whip my head around, only to encounter the wind howling through the open archways on the upper floors. They were probably windows once; the remnants of crystal lay on the ground where it landed after falling from its rotting frame. It sparkles in the dark Fae gloom, shooting rainbows all around me.

Dry, cracked leaves roll across the floor skittering with the dust. My eyes pick out another set of newly disturbed dust prints. They end in an alcove hidden behind a rotting drape. My left hand runs over the leather covering my chest and closes on a handle.

I slide the dagger from its hiding place, positioning the curve of its small handle between my fingers.

Vibrations rise from my chest, popping the overburdened threads and freeing the drape. Like a heavy branch, it slumps to the floor and reveals two round eyes.

"Zoe," the whisper slips from my lips. "How did you get here? Why?" Blood pounds in my ears, screaming at me.

Zoe presses her lips flat, shaking her blonde curls.

I move in a flash to her side, kneeling down in front of her. Her body trembles, vibrating the bench and loosening dust motes to float in the air.

I turn my back to the wall, eyes searching the dark for signs of trouble.

"Sarah?" Zoe calls.

I nod without taking my eyes from the room.

"They took me, I stayed out too late." Her nose flares and tears roll down her cheeks creating dirt rivers.

"Come with me!" I pull at her hand, but she stays fast in her seat.

"I can't, they won't let me leave. I'm their toy. They can do whatever they want. There is no Queen, Fae is ruled by wild," she moans.

Boy was that true. Everyone here runs wild and crazy for sure.

I yank at her arm, but her body is super glued in place. "You can never leave this place, I'm the bait." A wicked laugh escapes her lips as they pull back into a withered skull, revealing all of her teeth.

I watched in horror as the creature that once appeared to be Zoe turns into a ghostly specter. It lifts into the air to tower over me and releases a chilling screech.

"I've got you now, Fae-ling. Oh, I shall be rewarded by wild," The wraith exclaims, and claps its hands together without issuing a sound. It dips and swirls around me, trailing scratch marks in its wake.

I flash back to the archway I entered from only to bounce off an invisible wall and land on my ass. *Awe, fuck.*

"I told you," she says in a sing-song voice. "You can't leave without my leave." her chalkboard scraping shrieks rebound around the cavernous room. "Dance with us, we get so lonely. You are the first living Fae we've seen since Jacques tried to seat Jill on the stone throne." She cackles.

Jumping to my feet, I examine the room in quick succession. The snickering and bellowing whips past me anew, pulling at my hair and clothes. I sing a few bars from Queen's One Vision, and the veil covering the phantasms falls, exposing a ballroom filled with the ghostly forms of one time Fae.

My eyes grow three sizes to take it all in. It is nothing more than a ghost party for the dead. Swirling around the room, each Fae more decadent than the last. Tugging me left and right, their vapid hands are barely able to clasp a bit of my fleshy form. They tear at me for a dance and attention.

My heart beats through my chest and my hands become moist. I can't leave without their leave or permission?

That only leaves a bargain. I have to make one. What can you give the dead if you can't give them life? Relevance, revenge? What is their deepest desire?

"I want to dance with a prince, I've never done that before. Is there one here?" I inquire.

A deep baritone voice takes up my offer. "Of course there is a prince." The male Fae in front of me holds out his ghostly hand and I take it in my own; he becomes solid with my willing touch.

"You give me great pleasure with this dance. I am Barron," he announces, giving me a courtly bow and kissing the back of my hand.

I could just make out the shape of his lips as they graze the delicate skin. Then he pulls me into his arms and we float away on an unearthly dance floor, up into the rafters.

Barron quickly changes places with another Fae, then another and another. They shove each other out of the way for their turn.

"Stop tearing at her or there won't be enough left for everyone to have a turn," wails the Banshee who'd lured me.

She floats nearby, changing from a vision of Zoe to a crazed corpse in a rotting dress. Her hair sticks out around her like lightning bolts. The oculars of her skull are nothing more than black voids with a shiny silver marble suspended in the middle.

"Don't you like our ball? I thought this is what you wanted, a prince and a dance?" she demands while waving her arms around and spinning in a circle.

The newest specter seizes my hand and my waist to turn me at a dizzying speed, wickedly close to the walls and minstrels' gallery. I come close enough to catch a glimpse of the magic wake covering the arched entrance.

"No, I don't want to dance with a prince at a ball, God. What am I, ten? I'm not looking for a white knight I just want to get out of here," I retort.

She throws her head back and gives what I can only describe as a cackle. "You may not leave without my leave," she sings it from across the room.

"What do you want? Don't *you* want to leave this place?" I yell over my latest partner.

"I want to rage across the moors and lure men to their deaths," she cackles on.

"I can't offer you that, but I can get you out of this room," I reply cautiously, turning my head to keep an eye on the Banshee.

"You can't even get yourself out, how could you possibly help us?" She shouts, floating closer.

"I didn't say everyone, just you," I explain, then huff as my latest partner pulls me out of a dip and twirls my bangs in my face. Puffing air from my lips, I push my hair out of the way.

She moves in next to me, shoving my partner out of the way and taking over. "Why would I forsake my brethren on the word of a Changeling. All of Fae knows how fickle your kind can be," she whispers low, then finishes with a cackling laugh.

"Fickle? You've got it all wrong, lady. Fae are fickle, but *I'm* making you a deal. Give your leave and we can both leave." I stare her down, unblinking.

Dropping me like a rock, I get an up close and personal on the parquet floor as my face smashes into it. The taste of dust is on my tongue and in my lungs, and can only be expelled with a cough.

"Did you hear her? She wants to make a deal to let one of us out. Who here would turn on the other? We have been trapped here for so long, how many Queens have passed? How can you possibly believe we will turn on each other for freedom?" she shouts her reply, which is followed by a deranged cackle.

It doesn't matter what I believed, but what they believed. Divide and conquer, that is all I'm looking for.

"I give this one-time offer." I swallow and take a deep breath. *God, I hope this works.* "I will be Queen and when I am, I'll free only one of you. What do you have to lose? If I fail, you will still be here, but if I win, one of you can leave." I finish with my head held as high as possible. I wanted to look strong and regal, like a modern-day Cleopatra, or Elizabeth I. They ruled their countries with dignity and never backed down. Of course, Cleopatra did commit suicide, and Elizabeth died alone of old age or lead poisoning—not sure which but they ruled. In a time when only men ruled, they managed to do it.

I'm not Fae or human, but in a world where only Fae rule, I will rule.

I wait and try not to hold my breath or fidget. The image of Janice standing still as a statue in Deston's rooms near the fire lights my mind and I try to emulate it. The still of the Fae in the ballroom settles over me.

A slow muttering in the far-off corners grow and become a mumble, then a low quibbling. I desperately want to turn my head and find the source of the conversation, but I don't want to look too eager.

"How will you free one of us, changeling?" the demanding voice of a ghoulish Fae finds me.

"I am almost all Fae, I bleed blue and make mushrooms. When I sit on the throne, my change will be complete. I will have all the power of a full Fae Queen to call on. Need I say more?" The ash in my mouth fills me with the bitter taste of truth.

My humanity is almost gone; if there *is* any left it can't be more than a drop. Heat pricks behind my eyes and rolls in my belly. As sure as the sun will rise on the surface, the throne will take that last drop of my humanity, leaving only Fae behind.

I swallow back the rock in my throat for a clear retort.

The room roars to life, then screaming and gnashing of long-forgotten teeth tear around me along with the specters, each one scratching at me as they dive-bomb.

I stand my ground, unwilling to give even an inch against their onslaught. The hum starts in my throat and grows to encompass my chest, radiating around my form. It continues out, creating a bubble of protection.

"Tell me what you are!" I demand, pulling the full force of charisma and compulsion, bending it to my will, and then blasting it out to fill every nook and cranny.

A keening whips around the cavernous room, bouncing off walls and cracking crystal panes, causing them to crash to the floor and shatter.

The Banshee wails with her sheer hands covering the ghostly outline of what was once her ears.

"I am Banshee, they are Sluagh. I will free you, but you cannot free one of them without the others. They are one and separate, a swarm of death. The leftover souls of humanity that were never buried on sacred ground." Her ghostly form slumps to the floor, clawing through the solid surface.

"Give me your leave!" I demand with a pounding heart, as they tear through that air around me trailing cuts across my body.

"My Queen, you have my leave, now please make it stop. I will serve as you wish in all things. I swear my fealty to you." She lays her head on the parquet floor in supplication.

A reverberating boom wakes across the space like a wave working its way around an island. The Sluagh begin their onslaught anew. Now they aren't taking turns but instead working in teams. Three and four at a time rip at me from all sides, desperate to shred my clothes and skin.

They form a wall of screaming, soulless phantasms, each mouth open to a vacant void.

I rumbled my protection into a driving wall, batting them out of my way heading to the closest archway.

As I step into another corridor, a magical boom follows behind me. I turn to watch in horror as the Sluagh tear at the Banshee, ripping her ghostly parts and tossing them against the walls with a bang.

I tried to reach through and pull her with me, but the protection wall held firm. I pound with both fists, and I wince at the terror-filled eyes of the specter before they began to chew on her various parts.

Her lips moved and coughed out black ghostly blood. "You kept your word, my lady, I am free, of this place." The silvery light in her marble-shaped eyes dims and fades away.

Shuttering, I hurry down the hallway, checking the wake lines for trouble as I go.

CHAPTER 26

No matter how I try, to can't remove all the ghastly visions of death. My heart races with fear and loathing for the next grizzly encounter.

My own words ring over and over in my mind. With the seat, the last of my humanity will be gone, leaving only my Fae self.

Do I want that? Wants and desires are for people with no responsibilities.

The hall morphs into a pipe-shaped tunnel with a pinprick of light at the end glinting off damp, moldy walls. Wake lines edge the scene. The air is laced with a flavor I haven't encountered since Nick died, human and Red Bull.

Hysterical laughter rings through the pipe. "Awe, good things do come to those who wait," Nikki muses, her cheesy line.

Whipping my head left and right, I turn before pulling Silver, and then humming my protection spell.

"You really want to win, so why wait for me? You could have already made it to the throne, if you know where it is," I say, trying to goad her.

Her laughter told me all I need to know, she's completely cracked. A manic reply booms back to me, "I'm not going to take what is mine without killing you." She follows her words with a giggle.

Why do they have to all sound mad? Why can't I fight a nice normal monster? The wake lines of her illusion are as cracked as she is. Reaching out, I pull a few apart. Then, I watch as the magic disintegrates into mist, revealing a wide foyer which reminds me of Deston's entrance hall. Nikki stands by the giant double wooden doors that are covered in scrollwork and dead flowers.

The stale lemon verbena scent lingers in the air around us, matching the dead blossoms lining the walls.

Nikki's eyes roll through a thousand colors, and her lips line with a tight smile hinting at her further derangement. Her hair hangs loose and haphazard over her shoulders, arms limp at her side gripping her mercury-laced sword. The shiny liquid moves over the blade, glinting in the dim light. The only word that comes to mind is wild.

"If you just take the throne you can do what you want with me," I venture while buying time for my first strike. Crossing over, I step to one side, keeping Silver raised but casual.

"Nope, I want you first," she sings her reply with another giggle. Then, quick as lightning, she pulls a dagger and tosses it at me.

Tumbling to the side, I roll over still clasping Silver and jump back to my feet, light as a feather.

"It will take more than a butter knife to kill me, Nikki," I respond while humming the stone-shaped flower buds from the walls and pelting her with them.

She exclaims, "Ouch, you little bitch. What did Nick see in you? I can't figure out." Then, stomps at me, each step cracking the flagstone floor. The closer she comes the wider the cracks.

"Red rover, red rover, send Nikki right over," Nikki says, in a sing-song voice, then raises her sword and flashes to my side while slashing at my head, only to meet Silver as I deflect her first blow.

I flash to the giant doors and push them open a crack. I don't want to fight her, I just want to win.

"It's not that easy, Sarah, I'll be harder to win over than Nick. You can't fuck me." Nikki sneers.

Flushing at her accusation, I retort, "If you think Nick could be won you didn't know him. He wasn't a prize to win. He was a person!" I scream at her. The door behind me slams shut, and the force pushes me away.

Carried on the thundering sound from the door, come the words. "One at a time."

Flashing to Nikki's side, I engage her. Ringing metal cuts the air just before she kicks me in the side. I stumble, toeing up to regain my balance.

Nikki moves in behind me, but I whip around to face her in time to deflect a new line of attack.

"You're willing to stab me in the back?" I goad her.

"Turnabout is fair play. You and Nick stabbed me in the back, teaming up against me." Her voice cracks with pain, and anguish colors her aura. The pain of Nick's loss has unhinged her mind, driving her to blame someone—and that someone is me. "I will never bow to Nick's killer, never," She screams.

Bringing Silver up over my head, I slash down at her, telegraphing my move. The rumble in my chest pulls fallen debris from the surrounding room to move around us, limiting our movements.

Nikki bats them away with her hand and a baseball song. Then she sings a nursery rhythm for protection.

She can't create new magic, I'm stronger than her.

For the first time, I feel I can win without killing her. Under my breath, I whisper, "Submit".

Her eyes fog and clear, and she shakes her head. "What did you say? Fae tricks don't work on me," she says with a sneer.

But it almost had. Aqualis gave me fealty and power over water, but the air is so dry I can barely pull more than a sip from it. I need an upper hand, something other than music.

Nikki launches a new assault, slashing wildly and thrusting at any opening she can find.

I counter every blow she rains on me, but it isn't getting me any closer to that door. I hum a change to Silver, then grab a mid-sized dagger from my waist.

The rocks turning in the air freeze, then coalesce, reforming to resemble the shape of a curvaceous woman, *Ignus*.

"My sisters have urged me to help you," Ignus informs the room.

I wasn't sure who she was addressing and glance from Nikki and back to Ignus.

"Good. Burn her where she stands. I want to hear her scream as her flesh crackles and cooks," Nikki orders. The rolling color of her eyes makes me dizzy, but it is the cold smile curving her lips that shakes me to the core.

Ignus turns to Nikki. "I wasn't addressing you, you are ruled by wild." Then, turning her back on Nikki, she addresses me. "My lady, I have chosen. I swear my fealty to you and the end of wild's rule. I now put all the power of fire and rock at your disposal." The room booms with the sound of rocks crashing against rocks as she kneels and crosses her left arm over her chest with crossed fingers while bowing her head.

Heat blows over me a moment before Nikki strikes the side of my head with her foot. I stumble over, and the floor rises up to meet my hands and face.

The crack of stone on stone and a whiff of smoke followed by a screech is all I hear. I turn over in time to see Nikki's size-8 foot coming down at my head.

Balling my hands into fists and pulling my arms in close before rolling to one side, I open my left hand in readiness to pull a dagger, but instead of a knife, a flame appears.

My forward motion propels my body up into a crouching position. My eyes meet Nikki's a moment before I rear back and fling the fireball at her.

Nikki's eyes widen, and she sings a protection bubble as the fire engulfs the surrounding protection field. The fire dissipates around her after pushing her back five feet.

"You think I'm afraid of fire? I was in the lava cavern while you were running free on the surface with my brother." She leaps at me, and her bubble crashes into me, forcing me back into a wall.

The vibrations from my chest batter at her spell, creating cracks in the wake lines. When the last wake snaps, the full weight of Nikki's body slams into mine, knocking my head against the hard stone wall.

Nikki's lips pulled back in a crazed grimace. "Here we are, face to face at last."

Lifting my right arm, I shove her off- but she grabs my wrist in a vice-like grip and hammers my hand into the stone, forcing me to release Silver and watch as it clatters to the floor.

"You can't get away now," Nikki announces. Her eyes, color roll through the earthy shades of the rainbow as she releases an unearthly cackle. Her forehead collides with mine, cracking the back of my skull into the rock again and again.

Blood trickles down my face and into my right eye, burning with coppery salt.

Nikki laughs—her face mirrors mine with a bloody trail. She bares her white teeth and licks the blood hanging on her upper lip, pulling it into her mouth.

"Mmm, I love the taste of my enemy's blood, it is sweet. Didn't the Huns eat the hearts of their enemies?" She sniggers.

I see my chance. Kneeing her in the groin, I butt my head into her nose. A sickening crunch sounds, along with a piercing scream, and I'm free.

She hunches down, one hand cradling her face as the blue blood pours out of her hand.

I close and open both hands and they fill with fire a moment before I throw them. Repeating the process until she's surrounded by a ring of fire on the floor.

"Give up, Nikki, and I'll heal you. Then, I'll send you back to the surface," I plead.

"Why would I want to go back there? What for? Nick is dead and so are my parents. I watched them all die. Revenge is all I have left." She sucks the blood from her fingers and charges through the whirling flames and kicks me in the sternum.

I fall back on my shoulders and use the momentum to kip up and land a one-two punch. She dodges the third and fights back with another kick to my side.

Stumbling, I regain my balance and square off with her again, keeping my fists up to protect my face. She shifts her feet and hips to her left leg and raises her right to kick. I grab her foot and turn it, forcing her to the ground.

The rumble rises in her chest and she sings a nursery rhythm to soften her landing.

I sing the first bar of a Chainsmokers song and she crashes into the wall. The power of the words pour from my mouth.

Nikki sneers, baring blood-covered teeth, and charges me.

Singing the next few bars, I use the magic to smack her down to the floor. Then, it lifts her up and slams her down again. Changing a few words to fit my needs, I thrust her down into a hole created by my song and pull her back out.

Nikki regains her feet, and the music rises in her throat, but I can't locate the danger. A stone knocks the air from my chest breaking the spell of my song.

I catch my breath in time for Nikki's impact into my solar plexus, forcing the air from my chest again. We both crash to the hard floor, rolling over the top of each other.

My insides feel like jelly from the battering, but I can't give up now. Nikki gains the upper hand, straddling my chest and blocking both arms. With no way to defend my face, I can only watch the fists come at me pummeling my face.

I turn my head to the side, offering my previously damaged side up for the beating, hoping to keep my nose intact.

"That's right, take it," Nikki giggles her crazed enjoyment.

Kicking up, I smash my knee into her back, then twist, chucking her to the side. I roll on to my knees as my hand finds the hilt of Silver and I grip if for dear life. I lift the blade in front of me as Nikki runs into the end, burying it all the way to the quillons in her chest.

She coughs blood and her eyes clear as the enchantment of wild bleeds away with her life. "Nick." She whispers, with a tear before sinking to the floor limp.

Searing heat lights behind my eyes, burning away tears desperate to be freed. Biting my trembling lip, I reach over and close her lifeless eyes.

A necklace falls from her bodice to the floor and the heart-shaped locket snaps open to reveal Nick on one side and Nikki the other. The two halves of the heart are laid open before me.

Screaming in frustration, I hear Nick's voice ring in my mind pleading to save Nikki. I couldn't even do that. Nikki's hair covers part of her face: I push it back, smudging more blood across her face. My lips work back and forth as I swallow back the pain. It's my fault, I got them both killed. I should have tried to trap her in a protection bubble. Or pushed her through a portal to anywhere. Instead, I fought her... but why? I wanted to kill her for the same reason she wanted to kill me: Nick.

The pressure in my chest grows with my realization—I failed Nick for nothing. Killing Nikki won't bring Nick back. It was just another dead kid I should have saved.

Wrapping my fingers around the locket, I clasp it to my chest. Slipping the chain over my head, I let the locket rest between my breast. I can never forget; the price has been too high.

The heavy wooden door looms before me. Moving up to my full height, I kick the door open, using the force of my will to slam both sides open and into the walls before pausing to catch my breath.

Oh, I'm so fucked.

CHAPTER 27

The floor is littered with bodies. Twenty of us had started this journey, and I know only one can win, but I wasn't prepared for the carnage on display or the creature seated at the far end in the stone chair. My head aches and itches. The skin around my skull burns.

The walls are lined on one side with high windows, allowing the dim Fae twilight to filter through and illuminate the Fae markings on the creature seated before me. Wooden chairs lay around the space in various positions, along with tables of all sizes. Walls shimmer with the silver of dead wood and crystalline flowers. In the center stands a circle of stacked stones, which appears to be a well. Behind the throne, a mural reaches from the floor to the ceiling, depicting a Queen with a creature similar to the one seated in front of me.

The creature stands up and opens its arms; in one hand he holds a torc, and in the other a snake. The snake turned its head, tasting the air with its forked tongue. It isn't a man, or a beast. Everything about it resembles Fae, and his head holds the most spectacular set of antlers I've ever seen, while his lower half is covered in fur. His legs are turned at an angle resembling a stag, only to end in cloven hooves. The only word that comes to mind is Satyr.

He smiles, revealing sharp white teeth, "Have you come to take your seat as Queen?" The leaves covering his upper body flex with the vibrations of his voice. A magical sound wakes out from him, dark and deep as the caves the Fae had hollowed out for a home.

My head tilts back as I take in his height while trying to meet his eyes, but they dart around the room like a wild animal changing color as they go. Even his leaves change from deep green to golden yellow. The room morphs with him, from the calm green to angry reds and cold gray in a constantly changing cycle.

"I'm here to end the Fae's reign of death. Who are you?" I respond, gritting my teeth and baring them to seem fierce. It's a cover for the quaking in my bones. He towers over me by more than three feet.

His magic wake surrounds me, black and unruly with the sharp edges of a spear.

"You cannot end death, little one. Death is and will always be. Just as *I* am and will always be." His leg lifts, kicking a broken table aside and shattering it against the wall.

Swallowing, I clear my throat. "Who or what are you?" My voice quivers.

"I am known by many names. The Green Man to some, Pan to others, wild, but my true name is Cernunnos. I am King here, and I rule." His last words came out deep as a dark cavern, hard and cold as the granite he was seated upon. His aura too is cold and black.

Shit.

Janice didn't breathe a word about this guy. What the fuck am I supposed to do now?

Cernunnos let the snake slide from his grasp on to the floor. It coils in on itself, raising its head, then it lets out a hiss and flashes its fiery red eyes.

The snake opens its mouth wide and pulls its forked tongue deep into its gaping maw, fangs dripping with venom. The snake rears back its chest growing before shooting venom across the room. I dive out of the way before it hits me. The venom puddles where I last stood and smoke rises all around it.

The last thing I need is to be melted with acid again. Humming a bubble around the viper, I lock it inside.

"You are twice as clever as your competitors, Changeling." Cernunnos' the deep bass of his voice vibrates through to my bones. It carries powerful wakes, to subtly push you to the edge. They burrow into my psyche, twisting in my mind.

The rumble in my chest rises to push it back, but the magic holds me hostage with its power. I can create cracks in the magic but not conquer it.

"Oh, don't fight, little Changeling, wild will always win. Your human half is so easy to turn. Humanity is naturally wild, they long for it. They were created by it." He walks around me, sniffing and shifting like a wolf teasing its prey.

He raises a staff with a stone set in the end. It glows a deep vermilion red, its inner light pulsing like a heart. As it comes level with my chest, a wrenching pulls at my heart.

"Yes, little one, let me take the magic from you," he softly whispers his intention with unexpected tenderness.

The tearing in my rib cage shakes my limbs. My eyes roll around in my head, and I can feel the loss of control beginning to consume me.

Fire shoots from one hand and water from the other; I can't control my magic. But the magic is defending itself. Wind blasts my hair back from my brow, filling my ears and mouth down into my lungs. It feels as though I might burst with the pressure.

A wispy voice flows over me. "My lady, I swear by the light of Fae and all I am, fealty to you. I give over the power of air to command as you see fit. Use it to push back wild, use it now for the love of Danu and all that is living." As quickly as Aer had come, she vanishes again and the pressure releases.

Exhaling, I blast Cernunnos against the wall, knocking the staff from his grasp.

"You think the elements can save you? You are nothing more than a Changeling," Cernunnos breathes out his reply.

"My mother was a Changeling, but I am so much more Fae than I ever was human," my response booms out, pushing Cernunnos back into the wall.

He jumps clear of my verbal blast zone. An itching vibration issues from his chest and his staff flies to his hand.

"Shall we start again?" Cernunnos raises both eyebrows questioningly.

Humming my protection bubble close to my skin, I free a dagger for my left hand then tighten my grip on Silver.

"Yeah, let's dance, freak!" I let the rumble begin picking up debris and swirl it like a storm. The storm moves around me, never touching even a hair on my head. Fighting in the chaos is my favorite battleground.

Cernunnos rumbles his own protection field. Using his staff, he blasts rocks into dust as they come at him. In a flash, he is by my side and raising his staff for his next attack. I pull the wake lines protecting him apart with a line from a Tom Petty song my mom liked and stab at his torso.

"Two can play at this game, little one," he roars, then baring the sharp incisors in his mouth. His teeth-rattling vibrations take my shield down and rocks pelt me.

Humming a counter, the rocks change their direction to hammer Cernunnos. Then, I slash at him again, only to meet the stone hardwood of his staff.

He blocks Silver, then whirls the staff around and hits me across the back. Then just as quickly he twirls it back and thrusts the end into my belly, doubling me over.

I stumble down on one knee with the unexpected impact of the blow. Then, rolling to one side, I jump to my feet just outside his reach.

He smiles and entreats me, "You have talent, but not enough to win. Let me take the magic you were never meant to have. I will free you from it." His voice softens at the end, and charisma oozes from between his lips.

The desire to give in to him blankets me and I falter.

Biting down on my lower lip, I savor the mind-sharpening pain. "Is that how you freed them?" I demand, crouched and ready for the next hit.

"They were too weak to survive. But you are strong, you may yet live." His reply is heavily laced with charisma, but the wakes no longer affect me.

The bodies on the floor are covered in cuts and slashes. Each has bloody trails coming from their eyes, nose, mouth, and ears. Most of the blood can't grow even one mushroom. The few mushrooms that did grow were small and white, or brown.

None resemble the mushrooms my blood grows, green and purple, and large enough to fill this room or my own forest.

Flashing around the room, I pop from one side to the other, one step ahead of the demon stag. But Cernunnos knows all these tricks. I flash one step below the stone chair, and he appears right in front of me, raising his staff. I flash across the room, popping in and out, but he keeps me from reaching the stone seat with every move.

To win, I need to change the playing field from his turf to mine. I begin singing, and when I reach the refrain about a dark horse I allow our eyes to meet. Cernunnos bellows. The power of it pushes me back, causing dust to filter down from the ceiling while shaking the stones.

"You will not mention that animal in my presence. Puca cannot interfere here." Cernunnos flashes to my side, and his meaty hand snatches at my hair.

I clumsily bat his hand away with my dagger, drawing blood. It drips on the stone and grows a large toadstool with a red top and white speckles.

Raising his staff, he prepares to attack me again. But the rumble in my chest morphs the wooden handle into a willow branch and the red stone is left hanging encased in the tangled willow leaves at one end.

Cernunnos hums it into a whip, gripping the red stone tight in the palm of his hand, then pulls the thin tip behind his back before flicking to forward to sting my face.

"I can turn you into an ugly troll or you can give me the magic." He flicks the willow whip left and right, allowing it to crack each direction.

I call on earth, and the stone walls move, shifting like puzzle pieces floating different directions. I waver on my feet as the stone I am perched on lifts, along with half the floor.

His willow whips out, wrapping around my neck. As my stone rises it pulls tighter, choking off my air. Sawing into the branch with my dagger, I hack at it until the end comes free.

Coughing, I rub the back of my hand across my throat to ease the pain away.

My best defense is a moving playing field—it keeps me on my toes, movement is life. I jump two stones over, not far above his head, and thrust Silver down at his large back.

Cernunnos turns his head and the giant rack on his head turns with him, wrenching Silver from my grasp. I cry out as it clatters to the ground.

"You've lost," his deep voice bellows, vibrating my bones. He lifts his cloven hoof and stomps down, shattering the magic holding the quicksilver in check. I watch in horror as the silver liquid slips between the cracks in the floor, melting back into the earth it had been pulled from.

My chest heaves and tears threaten to overflow. Silver had become my trusted form of defense. The hilt lay on the ground blade-less and dull, through my fingers still ache to grip it in my hand.

Cernunnos flashes to my side, plowing his fist into the side of my face while I am distracted. I fall like a feather drifting on the wind before slamming into the soft earth of the floor.

Cernunnos gazes over the side of the large stone he squats on. Feeling for the last dagger housed in my thigh sheath, I wrap my fingers tightly around the handle and flash next to the stone chair.

"No, little one, not this time." Cernunnos appears in front of me, just as I knew he would. I slash from right to left and left to right, creating an X from his shoulders to his belly. It's enough to weaken him.

He staggers back, and I move forward and stab at his belly. The dagger would never pierce the muscles on his chest enough to reach his heart.

A vice-like grip on the back of my head squeezes, pulling me off balance. But I spy the red stone jewel in his other hand glowing with my heartbeat.

"You're the reason the Queens fade. You kill them," I remark.

He releases a chuckle. "You are a clever Changeling. However, intelligence won't save you."

The crushing pull on my chest begins again in earnest. Wyld pulls at the edges of my mind, turning my instincts against me. The only desire I can feel is the need to flee from danger. Adrenaline rushes through my veins, feeding my fear and shaking my hold on my mind further.

The jewel siphons my magic away. I hone in on the only belief I can find. A real Queen can survive for a while at least. The stones' pull must work both ways.

Cernunnos' aura wakes the black of betrayal. Blinking back the black spots taking over my vision, I can make out the spell working on him. It emanates from the torc hanging on his antlers.

I pant to push back the pain shooting out from my heart. My beating pulse works like a pump, forcing the magic out of me and into the ruby jewel. The nerves along my skin send pain messages to my brain, singing my death.

The tears I was holding back pool and drip over the edge of my eyes to run down the sides of my face back into my hairline. I want the pain to stop, and one last chance to see my parents and Arty. Janice's violet eyes light my mind along with our one kiss. What would Janice say? He would tell me not to fight like a human. Squeezing my eyes shut, I can still feel the vibrating from Cernunnos' magic sucking every drop of mine dry.

I pulled a rabbit from a hat every time before, was it dumb luck?

"That's it, little changeling, give me the magic," Cernunnos dark voice wakes over me. His ancient magic eats mine as if I am nothing more than a bag of potato chips.

The challengers would need to keep coming until someone kills him and takes his place.

Puca's words play through my head alongside Janice's: don't think like a human, don't go for the obvious answer.

I don't need to kill him.

Blinking to clear my vision, I search the wakes surrounding him for the spell— there had to be one. But as my magic fades, so does my Fae ability to see it.

Pulling the last of my strength to me, I flash to a stone slab floating close to the door. There, lying next to Nikki is her sword. Pulling it from her death grip, I flash again.

"We were almost done," Cernunnos bellows.

Wiping the tears from my eyes, my hand comes away covered in blue blood. The floor where Cernunnos was pulling away my magic is covered in mushrooms.

The energy vial in my pouch is my last hope. I flash, hopscotching around the room as I rifle around for the tiny bottle. Pulling it from the bag triumphant, I pop the top and suck the golden drops of jet-fuel down my gullet to feed my body and shift into my next gear.

My eyes refocus, heightening what Fae is left in my blood. Tightening my grip on the vial, I flash again. The next stone I land on is close to the seat, and Cernunnos appears next to me. Tossing the bottle in the air, I push it next to the torc and hum to shatter it.

Cernunnos rears back and the torc slips from the tip of his antler. Humming the 'come to me' notes, I watch as it lands in my hand.

The wakes from the torc reach out to Cernunnos demanding its return.

"You must return my crown," he pleads, for once weak and vulnerable.

"Give me back my magic!" I respond. Calling on fire, I blast a lava puddle in the next stone and wave the torc over the burning liquid pool.

"No, if you destroy it Fae will fall." The lie rolls off his tongue so easily. He holds out the ruby jewel as an offering.

"Toss me the gem," I demand, letting the torc slip over my hand and down my arm. The red stone rises in the air and I pull it into my hands.

It beats with a heart all its own. Humming, I pull the magic to me. The realm of Fae opens in my mind's eye, revealing all. I flash to stand next to the stone seat.

"Don't! You will regret it, all who take the stone chair do. The ruby is a way out for a tired Queen," Cernunnos explains. The wake of lies follows his every word.

Pulling all the magic held in the stone, I devour it like a drug addict. It isn't just mine, but the power of every girl who entered the room and the old Queen. All our magic rolled into one big hit of magical crack. Power radiates from the gem and into me.

It had worked like a straw, sucking the power away from one and giving it to another. I can also use it to weaken my enemies. For a moment, I want to keep it and use it against all who would stand against me, like Deston. The aching around my skull grows to epic proportions, as does the pressure around my spine. The thirst for that kind of power sits at the tip of my tongue, tempting me with its sweet intoxication.

My eyes search all around the room. I wave my arm and the stones fall back to their homes in the walls and floors leaving only dust motes lingering in the air. My eyes land on Nikki's corpse. I'd killed her for a prize— this prize. The stone is red with the blood it had stolen from all the girls lying on the flagstones. Each had reached for the seat in front of me, and all had failed.

I close my hand over the beating rock, heat wakes from the facets pulsing in time with my desire to keep my prize. A cold certainty steals over me, for it would, in the end, destroy me. I squeeze until it shatters, sending shards into the granite chair and surrounding walls. Rumbling, I pulverize the pieces into dust and blow them away to the farthest reaches of the Hallowed Hills.

"Never again will one Fae steal what belongs to another." I take a step toward the cold seat before me, only to collide with an invisible wall.

Cernunnos slams his staff into the side of my head, knocking me off balance.

Stumbling, I flash out of range. The pounding in my head grows while blood slides down the back of my neck, causing the itching on my back to grow with my newfound magic.

Cernunnos flashes to my side. "Give me the torc and I'll allow you to leave this room alive," he demands. Lies, every word—he reeks with rage over what I've done. The stone is a drug, and he is an addict with no way to get a fix. He raises the wooden staff once again, minus the red jewel, to attack. I draw one of the chairs from the floor and slam it into his side.

Thrusting my hand out in front of me, I open a portal revealing the kitchen in my old house. Reaching through, I grab the first thing my hand lands on—the fire extinguisher—and pull it through.

With one swift motion, I hammer it into Cernunnos' sternum and pull the safety pin, angling the hose at his hunched-over form and squeeze the release valve. The nitrous pushes the white, powdery foam from the canister, filling Cernunnos' face and mouth.

He chokes, sweeping his staff left and right while searching for his target. But I jump to a new stone and open a new portal to the mushroom forest, then step through, groping, the loamy ground for a weapon other than Nikki's sword. My fingers trail over a buckler and a short sword. I clutched both, then the leap back into the throne room.

Cernunnos vibrates for rain, but I block his call, morphing it into hail, then I watch as it beats down on him. He swings the staff wildly at any noise I make as I flash next to him and slash with the short sword. His staff connects with the buckler, knocking it loose. I flash to a new position before the buckler clatters against the stone below.

Finally, his vision clears and he flashes to square off with me. "You may produce a portal, but it will not save you." He words ring hollow. He angles his staff on a collision course with my short sword. The hard wood of his staff cracks the metal of my blade, leaving me holding a jagged-tipped hilt.

Tossing it away, I flash to a new flagstone floating by the windows and open a portal to the bathroom in the cottage in Athens. Without taking my eyes from my opponent, I pick up the Khan 380 my father had given me hum a spell over it.

The pounding in my head reaches an epic proportion, causing my vision to blur. I flash to the stone seat and swallow back the butterflies in my chest.

Cernunnos stands between me and the only way to end this. Raising the gun, I take aim as he appears in front of me and I squeeze. The bullet penetrates his chest, throwing him back into the seat. I watch the deep blue blood of his life pump out on to the floor around my feet. His form slides down the granite seat, antlers raking over the hard stone until he finally slumps at my feet.

Coughing, he remarks, "Alice, I was such a fool. I didn't mean to kill the stag, Deston tricked me." His admission sounds so human.

Dropping the gun, I crouch down to add pressure to the wound and slow the blood flow. The torc on my arm burns when it touches Cernunnos skin.

The taste of evil wakes from the so-called crown. The wake lines are sharp and digging into Cernunnos, reminds me of Puca's horse belts. Plucking one strand, then another, I pull the spell's hold apart, one note at a time. My voice rises with a song I've never heard before, ripping the torc's hold over the Fae before me.

As each string falls away, so does his enchantment. The antlers snap and wilt away, and his legs turn into the long, straight thighs of a man with feet and toes, leaving behind only a cloth to cover his manhood.

I pant—the effort of destroying this spell is taking more than I knew I could give. The last of the spell slips away, leaving only the shining torc in my hand pulsing with power.

Cernunnos' eyes clear to a deep moss green, and his face softens into a normal Fae. "Puca stole my Alice away from me." I freeze in place.

Alice, Puca, was he talking about my mother?

"Allison?" I whisper, holding my breath.

"Alice, my sweet love. Puca took her away from me. You look like her," He muses and coughs blood.

Placing my hands on either side of his face, I sing with all my might and watch as the sucking hole in his chest closes and his breathing strengthens. His eyes droop with the energy I pull.

The ripping pain in my back crests with the music. My head screams.

When I finally let the music drift away and the magic dies, the Fae lying before me is sleeping with deep and easy sighs.

Waving my hand, I disintegrate the toadstools surrounding us and hum Cernunnos up into a bed that forms at my will, placing him gently on the petal-soft covers and a pussy-willow pillow.

Turning my attention away from the sleeping Fae before me and back to the slab that beckons, the invisible wall blocking my claim gone. Turning around, I face the room and with shaking limbs sit.

All at once a massive wake waves out from my point, and a ripping pain in my back tears open the humps residing there; a wet wind moves over my shoulders. Screaming in agony, I grip the armrest and my head rears back. I'm forced to lock my jaw down on the convulsing affliction taking over my being.

A crushing pressure warps my mind and my vision. Grabbing the sides of my skull, I encounter thorns-shaped horns protruding all around the back and side. The sharp tips curved in to face the center of my pate, dividing my hair into sections hanging between what had become a thorny crown.

The wake of torment arches away from me, clearing my eyes as it goes.

In the center of the room in the stone well blooms the flower I'd made with Janice. It finished blooming into an ebony black poppy and the sharp thorns angle out around the velvety petals, defending its delicate beauty.

A groan drifts from behind reaching me, and I turn to catch a glimpse of Cernunnos, but instead watch in amazement as wings flutter at my back. I whistle up a mirror just the way Lavender taught me, holding the last note longer than usual to increase size.

The scrolled wooden frame reveals my black hair sectioned off by glossy white, razor-sharp horns in a horseshoe shape around my head, and a set of misty green gossamer wings at my back, leaving wide golden eyes. Rearing up and pivoting on a dime, I stare at the mural behind me.

There, on the wall, is a Queen with golden hair and golden horns, the outline of wings at her back and her hand held by a black hair man with golden eyes. He carries a set of horns, too, and the legs of a satyr. It was the smile dancing over his lips that gives him away: Puca. He had been King, but he lives?

CHAPTER 28

"Yes, it's me. You chose well, Granddaughter. I knew you would. Only one choice left to make." Puca's sudden appearance shakes the room and me.

"How?" I whisper in awe.

"Love, she made me and named me Oberon, King, but she was betrayed. The new Queen took the throne, freeing me. Being King changes you. I am not ruled like the rest of Fae. I am free." Puca smirks and saunters up to my chair snatching my hand, he lays a gentle kiss on it and steps back.

"Why does Cernunnos hate you, and who is Alice?" I inquire with bated breath.

Puca cocks an eyebrow and crosses his arms. "He hates me? Humm, I didn't know that. I'm surprised." He flashes both rows of white teeth and uncrosses his arms. "That rarely happens for me but is the norm when dealing with you or your mother. I helped Alice escape, your mother, Allison, Alice. We changed her name several times to protect her. Being the daughter of the once king of Fae is a dangerous thing." In true Puca style, he prances around the room, searching the faces of the fallen.

He stops and lingers over Nikki, pushing the hair back from her fiercely beautiful face. His hand trails down to her chest to the mortal wound. His aura never changes, but the sorrow oozes from him. He coughs before returning to stand near my chair. "I liked this chair so much better when it sat in a meadow before Jillian lost us the surface and built this awful monstrosity." He sighs with longing.

Taking a deep breath, I ask the question Puca is skirting in his oh so irritating fashion. "Who is Cernunnos to my mom?" I hold the air in my chest.

"Well, your father, of course. Who did you think? You really should spend a little more time paying attention to detail instead of fighting against it. Or you could go ask your mother, but that might be a bit awkward with your 'dad' around, humm?" He turns on one foot to leave.

"Where are you going?" I demand in confusion.

Throwing a glance over his shoulder, he says "You don't rule me, child. I go where I may. All of Fae will come to congratulate you and kiss up to you. Remember, however, that I was first, and don't make the obvious choice. I'll see you around, your Majesty." Puca winks and makes to step through the portal he'd called.

"Who betrayed your queen?" I demand.

His head lowers a fraction of an inch, but he never turns. "You already know, you've been told the story and met the fiend. Jacques, Jack." He sighs.

"But Jacques failed, and broke his crown," I remark.

Puca turns, leveling both golden eyes on me. "No, Jacques broke the *Fae* crown. Jillian fell much later when her king betrayed her. She tumbled after. What do they teach you these days? Fairytales are our history." He throws his hands up in exasperation and steps back into his cottage, allowing Lavender and Janice to pass through the portal back to me.

Lavender bows deeply along with Janice. "My lady, I offer my services," Lavender announces, her head remaining down.

Janice coughs, tilting his head up a bit so I can see his violet eyes glance from Lavender to me.

"May I rise?" Lavender asks.

"Oh, sorry, you, you may rise," I stutter.

She rises and comes to my side, singing a cleaning song.

"Leave it, I want all of Fae to see," I order.

She whispers, "My lady." Then, she nods at Janice who still bows at the base of the stairs.

"Pl… rise, Janice" I stammer.

"My lady, do you wish to clean the room before your subjects arrive?" Janice inquires and turns slightly to indicate the bodies on the floor.

"No, I wish for every Fae to see what deceit has cost," I reply, humming. Then, I release a power I never knew could exist and watch as the vision of my mind takes form in front of me.

The bodies of the fallen challengers lift and reposition themselves before lowering to a row at the sides of the room, floating like the carved effigies of the Knights Templar.

It is all I can do to keep the lump in my throat at bay and the tears in their place. Seven bodies line either side, with Nikki floating in the center closest to my throne.

The room morphs around me, adjusting to my whim. The walls are laced with flowers, and light from Fae shines through clear windows, illuminating the floors and walls. The mural behind me shines with renewed color, defining the golden age of Fae. It reveals the true contents of the scene when all was young and filled with hope.

The blood of the fallen lay in puddles around the room. The largest and the only one with mushrooms is at the entrance to the throne room, Nikki's.

I can't bring myself to leave my seat, even with the tears threatening. I won't cry in front of Fae.

Using measured steps, Janice approaches my throne. "Your Majesty, will you allow me to heal you?" Fear and longing wake from him. His aura colors with uncertainty.

"Please don't call me that. Sarinah is my real name. Please, call me Sarinah or just plain Sarah," I plead with a tentative smile.

Janice reaches my side, only to kneel at my feet. I don't want him subservient to me. "Please don't treat me different, Janice, I can't take it." I cup his chin lifting his face to mine, and find a fine layer of hair covers his cheeks.

His voice rises, carrying love on every note and wiping the aches and pains away. I drown in his violet eyes. Without a moment's hesitation, he leans in and our lips meet. My heart speeds up as a new fire tears through my veins and just as quickly we part.

"I love you," I whisper.

The smile I always long for spreads across his face. In a husky voice, he replies, "I love you too, but you already knew that." His hand caresses my neck and his forehead touches mine.

I choke back my laugh. "Well, you have to love to heal. Puca explained how it works."

Lavender cuts in, "Your Majesty 'they' come—the Princes."

Janice releases me and turns to leave.

I call to him, "Don't! stay by my side!" My hand grips his while the other hand grips the armrest whitening my knuckles.

Janice's response is quick and measured, "Sarinah, I will from this day forward stand wherever your heart desires." His brows draw together. "But this once I must decline. It is the only time you must face this on your own. It is the only way they will respect you.”

I hear the wisdom in his words and huff a sigh. My hand lingers until our fingertips pull apart. He steps back and takes up a position off to the side.

Lavender moves around the room, primping the dead.

“Don’t clean the blood from them, just fix their hair and makeup. I want them to look as beautiful as possible. I don’t want all of Fae snickering about their looks.”

Four figures approach the great arched doorway, each in step with the other. Two of white and two of black, each dressed to kill.

Jacques enters with Deston at his side, while Bonn and Wot keep to each other. They stride to the base of the dais and bow in unison. I let them hang there for a moment too long, just because.

“You may rise!” I order.

The Princes raise their heads in turn. Deston’s eyes bore into me, but I ignore his feeble attempts to ensnare me with charisma; I’m beyond that level of control. Jacques carries an air of disdain while covertly searching the great room for something. His eyes trail across the prone form of Cernunnos, and a small cruel smile edges his lips.

Bonn and Wot wait with eager smiles.

Bonn opens his mouth, only to be cut off by Deston saying, "Where is our King?" Deston's eyes wander the large space, lingering on the form of Cernunnos off in the corner. From Deston's vantage point with all the blood, Cernunnos could be dead.

"Is that all you have to say to your new Queen?" I inquire, drawing his attention back to me.

Deston's ears redden; he opens his mouth and quickly closes it again.

Bonn cuts in, "Your Majesty, the Seelie court rejoices with your ascension and weep for your fallen comrades." Bonn tilts his head down and crosses his fingers before touching them to his forehead. His wakes are clean and free of deceit. After a moment of silence, Bonn continues, "Won't you allow the Seelie court to care for the bodies of the fallen? I would be pleased to personally see your will fulfilled."

I'm taken aback at the good manners of the Seelie court. I didn't think Fae had any.

I reply, "I will handle the dead myself, but thank you. Is there anything else you would like to offer me?" Fealty—that is what Janice said I need.

Wot knelt to the floor, crossing his fingers, and tilts his head down. "I will swear my fealty to you." Wot's words and actions are echoed by Bonn.

"I accept your pledge, in the name of Danu and Oberon," A half smile quirks my face. Just evoking Puca's name makes me want to laugh. "The first King and Queen of Fae. Arise and be recognized." Both regain their feet and step to the side to reveal additional Fae gathering in the outer reaches of the grand room.

Jacques frown deepens, along with Deston's barely contained rage.

Jacques raises his eyebrows as if he's just thought of something and spouts, "May I be the first to kiss your hand, my Queen?" He moves forward.

I raise my hand in a sign to stop. "Sorry, Charlie, but you ain't the first. Someone beat you to it. Perhaps you'd like to swear your undying fealty instead?" I cock an eyebrow at him.

He steps back and turns his head to the side to spy the size of the audience, then smacks his dry lips together. "I cannot recognize your ascension without a king." He stares me down with his misogynist attitude.

I gasp. "You refuse to recognize my right to rule without some stupid man at my side? Are you kidding me?" The walls pale with my anger, and the wood turns the dry silver of death. Flowers fade from the walls, and leaves fall as if under an autumn breeze.

Both princes fall to their knees under the pressure. They strain to stay upright. "If you will not bend a knee without a king, then I will provide you with one. Who do you suggest?" I demand. God, now I'm starting to sound like the Fae.

Deston takes the bait. "You should choose your heart's desire." He bows his head to hide a small smile.

I shift my gaze to Jacques and await his bright idea.

He clears his throat and plunges in. "A king should be held in high regard by his people. A leader among Fae, a warrior able to defend Fae and his Queen, someone you trust with your life." His eyes shift to Janice and back to me in a flash.

They are herding me to a choice. I shoot a glance at Janice, and he stares through me at the mural behind.

I respond, "That's it? Neither of you wants to be king?" Gripping the stone armrest, I lean forward.

Cernunnos supplies, "They don't wish to become Wyld." The soft, study voice comes from behind. "To be king is to be Wyld. If the Queen is reason and order the King is wild and chaos. They don't want to lose control."

My head whips around to meet Cernunnos' dark remarks. I had to kill Cernunnos to win the throne, they know this. Cernunnos rises to stand behind my throne.

A gasp comes from the crowd. I turn back to survey my new subjects and find the shocked member.

On the seat next to me lays the torc gleaming with a magical spell. I grip the torc in both hands, holding it up for all to see.

Jacques and Deston smile tentatively in satisfaction, and their auras' color is glee. I hum a slight change to the torc and it shines back with renewed power.

"Janice, can you," I pause and skip over the please, "come over here?" I ask.

He moves, stone-faced, and stands before me, then bows deeply. His aura colors red with fear but is also lined with love.

I want to put his fear to rest, but that isn't going to draw my enemies out and trap them. "Janice, do I have your fealty?" I ask.

"You know you do. I offer myself as King if you so wish." Janice's unflinching overture eases my fears.

I sift my attention from Janice to Deston. "A lowly warrior in your court, Deston, is willing to offer what you will not." I turn my gaze to Jacques. "Lavender, come before me," I order.

She comes out from behind the throne and takes up a position next to Janice. I continue, "Lavender, do I have your fealty?" I inquire.

Lavender lifts her head, giving me an easy smile. "Yes, always and for all time, my Queen," she replies, and her sight shifts from me to Cernunnos.

Not taking my eyes from Jacques, I continue, "Jacques, a member of your court offers me what you deny. What have you to say?" I demand, drumming my fingers on the stone chair.

Jacques never flinches, but stoically replies, "I gave this Fae to Deston at his request. I take no part in the choices of his court. I offer myself as king if you desire." He leans back, straining against the magic hold I place on him.

Deston is the patsy, Jacques' offering in case I don't take Janice. This was the plan all along. Jacques would never have given Lavender to Deston, as a favor. He kept Arty for insurance, only parading him out to show me he has something I want.

Deston's muscles work to hold him upright. He raises his voice in self-defense, "Sarah, Your Majesty, do not trust Jacques. He will betray you. It was his idea to throw you and Janice together. He hopes you will choose Janice, leaving us to manipulate you to his own ends." Deston's green eyes search my face in desperation. He fears being named King— he fears the crown more than anything.

Puca's words ring in my mind, 'Only one choice left to make, don't make the obvious one'.

"I offer myself as King, should you have need of me, your Majesty," Bonn announces and sweeps down into a deep bow.

Wot wakes fear and stumbles over his words. "I w-would be-e honored to be King, if you so desire." He tilts his head down to hide the fear etched on his face.

I had seen what being king meant, and I had them right where I wanted them. *Now to spring the trap.*

To rule is about control or the illusion of control. "Janice, and the princes of each court, come to me." I hold my breath as each Fae, in turn, took the steps to cluster in front of my stone seat.

Tilting my head back to take in the faces before me, I swallow. How do I make this work?

"I only wish for the strongest leader for our people." I know they don't consider humans our people, but I do. I can't choose anyone who wouldn't take my point of view. I pull a tight smile across my face.

I plunge in—it will work, I know it will. "If you can't give me your fealty, then offer me your hand in friendship so I can move our people into the modern world." I give a nervous laugh to throw everyone off.

Janice raises an eyebrow at me. I arch one in return, then thrust my hand out, palm up.

Janice covers my palm in an instant, then Bonn and Wot move to join with their own. The hands of each Fae closes around the meat of my palm reminding me not all of Fae is out to kill me. Just most of it.

Deston lays a flat palm over Wot's, joined by Jacques. In a flash, I move both hands to encase Deston's and Jacques' wrist in the torc of Kingship.

Bonn and Wot rear back, but I wake my will over them, forcing them into supplication on the flagstone floor. Janice steps back next to Cernunnos.

"What have you done?" Jacques sputters, his fear reeking from every pour as he yanks at his trapped arm.

"You fool, I told you she was bright for a changeling. Now you've killed us both." Deston's whining sours with his weak tears.

Both stumble back, and Deston trips on the top stair, tilting Jacques off balance. Jacques grabs the torc bracelet and pulls with all his might to dislodge his arm from the circle.

The soft tenor of Cernunnos normal voice reverberates from over my shoulder. "How does it feel, Jacques, to be trapped by Wyld? I don't feel the joy of conquest you felt when you trapped me. I never would have killed the white stag if I'd know it was our King. You tricked us all, but no more." Cernunnos closes his tired eyes, then opens them afresh. "You cannot know all the parameters of any equations. Mine was my child. She came to right all your wrongs. Behold Danu's revenge, your Queen Sarinah, my daughter, and granddaughter to Oberon himself." Cernunnos' words blast over the room with all the power of the once king of Fae.

I wait for the magic wakes to ease their changes. Then, I stand for the first time and leave the stone throne. I move up to the one-time princes of the realm and grab the torc and snap it in half.

Both princes instantly change, I listen to the pained cries as their legs turn back on themselves creating the cloven hooves of a stag. Fur rushes to cover the lower half of their torsos, while they bend in half with the forced growth of antlers. Each rack carries 14 points per side. When finally, the changes ceased, two heads raise, and both stare at me through the multi-colored eyes of Wyld. Their faces are covered with the leaves of the forest, ever changing with the seasons and weather. The deep baritone of a black cavernous cave reaches me when their mouths open.

"I swear to you my Queen," the echoed power of their fealty bounces around the space, thrusting Fae to the side with its superiority.

Wasting not one second, I say, "Behold your Kings, Jacques and Deston. They will hold the power of Wyld for all time. The deceit of Jack is over his hold over Fae broken. All who follow Jacques would be wise to let it go. I'll win, I always win— it is what I was born to do." I search the massive space and the many faces for Puca. He leans with his back against the doors, minus a shirt, but carrying a quiet smile of approval. He hitches his lips to the side in a half smile and gives me a mock clap.

The heavily crowded room falls like a wave to their knees in recognition. "I name Janice as Consort to the Crown and leader of the royal army." With my proclamation, the fuzz on Janice's chin grows into a double-braided goatee. "The human realm is closed to all Fae for all time. None may cross realms without my permission, save Puca. Brake this, and the punishment is an eternal test of iron and Fae. All humans are to be returned to the surface, save those with Fae in their blood. Changelings may choose to stay or go this one time." I let my pronouncement ring before taking my seat again.

Surveying the many faces of Fae present, I find Puca again amongst the crowd. He mouths, "Well done, my child." Then, he opens a portal to a space suspiciously like Sorenson's kitchen and is gone.

Lifting my hand to find Janice's in my own, I give him a grateful smile and turn to face the realm I'd won.

CHAPTER 29

Fae spend a great deal of their time on pomp and bullshit. I'd be happy if everyone who wants to swear fealty just took a knee all at once, so I could be done with it. They at least came in groups, offering congratulations or fealty. There's bored, and then there's wishing I could see my veins open with a rotting piece of wood.

At last, the Fae twilight creeps up to darken the windows. Janice claps his hands announcing the end of court.

Fae filter out the doors to wander the corridors and Lavender closes the great door with a solid thud.

Lavender's aura wakes exhaustion, every step compounding the weight. "Your Majesty, I have not had a chance to thank you for saving my brother." I watch in fascination as Cernunnos crosses the room and takes her hand. Cernunnos smiles down at her and back up at me.

"Alice left in such a hurry I was unaware of her state or her fear. She was right to leave taking you with her," he supplies.

Lavender's smile shines with gratitude.

I sputter, "This is the prince? Cernunnos? He's your brother?" I look from Lavender to Cernunnos and both nod in unison.

Cernunnos continues, "Our Queen threaten to rip all Fae from Alice's blood if she stayed. I tried to soothe her fears, but the day of the hunt she disappeared in the forest and I became wild."

I broke in, "But Lavender, you said Deston killed your brother."

Neither Jacques or Deston look dead to me. Both stand to one side of the throne still as a statue, staring off into nothingness. Wild consumes them for anyone to see, filling their eyes with a kaleidoscope of colors. They neither speak nor move of their own accord since I broke the torc.

I can see the magic waking between the two torc halves; its only desire is to become whole again.

Cernunnos' soft voice drifts to me, breaking into my thoughts. "To be wild is a death sentence, for when the queen fades the new cannot ascend while the king lives. Each king must be killed by the new queen."

I pale. "But I didn't kill you. You live. I pulled the spell's hold over you and healed you," I respond.

Cernunnos adds, "I would surely have died if you had not. What did you do to the torc before giving it to our new kings?" His face darkens at the reference to Jacques and Deston.

I remark with a shrug, "I made it bigger—it needed to slip over both wrists at the same time."

Janice leans over, laying a kiss on my temple, raising my heart rate and temperature. I smile up at him, and he returns it with one of those rare smiles I always long for.

Before I can take to my feet, a powerful down sweep of my wings lifts me from the hard stone. Concentrating, I slow the beating of my wings and lower myself to the ground, stumbling with unsure feet.

Smiling I remark, "I'll have to work on the landings."

We all laugh. For a moment happiness fills me before the reality of all the world had lost slams down on me. The bodies of the fallen still float nearby, and neither Nick or Arty can enjoy this moment with me.

I wave my hand, opening a portal to Jacques portico, nodding a farewell to Lavender and Cernunnos. Janice takes my hand and leads me through to the crowded space on the other side.

The UnSeelie court falls to their knees in obedience as Janice steps back.

The sea of multi-colored hair hides their allegiance. I breathe out magic, ripping the dye from them to reveal their true affiliation.

"I want every human delivered to the forecourt, all in the dungeons to be freed and sworn allegiance from all of you. The Hallowed Hills are closed for all time from the human-covered surface. You have one human hour." Without a look back, I turn and waltz into Jacques's throne room, taking the seat.

The walls wake back satisfaction, and I quirk a smile. They knew I'd win. Even though I could take this castle for my own, I won it fair and square. The thought of living here turns to ice in my belly.

I'm only here for one reason—Arty.

An hour could have been days, it drags on so long. Finally, I rise to survey the returnees. The forecourt is filled with humans, all enchanted and bedraggled.

Thrusting out my hand, I open a portal to my home town and sing away the enchantment, watching as many weep and run through to the human world. The numbers dwindle, along with my hopes.

A few linger, their blood laced with Fae and magic. "You are free to leave with the others or stay as you choose, but your choice is a final one." As I listen to myself, I sound like someone else—an older, wiser version of me. Not the eighteen-year-old kid I'd been when I blasted my way back into Fae.

One or two humans stay, leaving the forecourt with one Fae or another. The others leave together.

Arty is nowhere to be seen.

"Where is the human Jacques held named Arthur?" I demand of the seneschal.

He shakes his head and waking back fear.

I want to compel him, but that would make me no better than Deston or Jacques.

Janice whispers in my ear, "Offer them a boon for Arthur's safe return."

I nod and announce, "A boon of my choosing, for the safe return of Arthur, alive." I allow my eyes to linger over the castle. "If one hair on his head is damaged, however, I'll pull this castle down and leave only rubble behind." My throat closes and I will a portal to Deston's throne room.

Fae loiter on the steps and lean against the walls as I step through none move.

Janice clenches his jaw to bite down on his anger. "Bow for your Queen. This domain no longer answers to Deston. Only to Sarinah." Janice's proclamation sweeps over them like leaves blown from a tree. They fall, many crossing their fingers over their heart and bowing their heads.

Opening my wings, I take up my full height to dominate the inhabitance.

Same orders, different castle, until the members of the dungeon are marched out.

There, filthy and sickly thin stands a hunched form with milky green eyes and brownish black hair. I can see the human still lining his features, but much about him has changed.

I bite back the cry and the threat of a flood of tears.

Ending the enchantment over the human chattel causes a new rush to leave via the open portal. I point the way home, only to see three men left behind. They stand shoulder to shoulder.

I fear what I will say or do. Not wanting to look weak, I order. "Clear the room! leave only these two and my consort!"

The Fae flee like a rush of water sliding down a mountainside. None fall or trip only the perfect motion of escape.

Slamming doors, I close us off to the castle and the rest of the Fae world.

I flash to their sides and wrap my arms around two bulky forms. Shuddering, I try to suck in air, but the lump in my throat blocks everything beyond my cries.

With barely a whisper, I remark, "I thought you both were dead." The walls weep with me. My hands curl around Arty's neck and Nick's. They both laugh and speak at once.

"I didn't die, I was never there. Neither of us was," Nick's matter of fact reply comes with a half-smile.

Choking back my laugh, I pull them into another hug. I can't let go. "But I saw you, you wilted away." My eyes dart from Nick to Arty.

Nick shakes his head and replies, "It was all an illusion. I never left the dungeon. Jacques and Deston bounced me back and forth like a ping pong ball. I met Arty when Jacques showed up and Deston wanted to kill one of us."

Covering my mouth with my hand, I press back my fears.

Arty pulls his glasses out of his pocket to reveal a cracked lens. They sit crooked on his face. I didn't care, I was so happy to see his dirt-stained face and shy smile I couldn't stop hugging him.

Sniffing, I wipe the moisture from my eyes.

Arty smiles at Nick and shoves his shoulder into Nick's, then jumps in, "Yeah, I set him straight about just being friends. But it took you long enough. I thought you'd never get us out." Arty tilts his head to look down his nose at me, but it doesn't work so well anymore. "Did you get taller? And what's with the wings?" Arty pats the top of my head.

I pull them both in for a hug.

I don't want to break the mood, but some things have to be done. "Nick, I'm sorry I... I killed your sister." Taking a breath to steady myself, I continue, "I didn't want to, but she wouldn't let it go—she'd gone full-on cray, cray. She thought you were dead and I killed you. There's nothing I can say to make it right." I can't meet his eyes, so I stare at the floor.

The same floor I saw when Janice had first brought me to Fae and made me choose. Arty's big meaty hand claps my shoulder, squeezing. Then, it slides across my back into a side hug.

Nick steps away, sniffling, followed by a choking cry. I pull the locket from around my neck and offer it to him. Pulling out of Arty's grasp, I wrap my arms around Nick's shaking form. He weeps openly and sags into my embrace.

With a shaking breath, he inquires, "Was it quick?"

I whisper back, "Yes, she didn't suffer. You were her last thought. She wanted to avenge your death."

He nods his head into my hair and shudders, then pulls back. "Keep it, I have my own." He chokes on a new cry, then bites down on his knuckle before continuing. "We can both remember her." He pulls on a leather strip to reveal the mirrored locket hanging at the end.

Nick throws a glance at Arty, then back to me. Nick runs his fingers through his hair, moving it over his ears to reveal a point. I gasp and step back.

"When did this happen?" I demand.

Nick rubs the tears from his eyes, giving me a wan smile. "We weren't actually in the bubble with you, but that doesn't mean we didn't experience it. I felt myself die. I watched Nikki stab me. When I woke up, I could feel the magic. Then some shirtless dude with black hair and yellow eyes shows up in my cell and tells me to choose Fae or humanity. I said as long as you were here, then so was I." He pulls in a shuttering breath, "I saw Nikki, me dying didn't drive her over the edge. Everything did." He coughs, swallowing back new tears. "She was never going to win, I just wanted to take her home, but she was already gone. Nikki died with our parents on the surface. I just didn't know it." He chokes again.

Janice clears his throat. All three of us turn to face him.

"That guy, why's that guy here?" Arty yells. "He's the one that took us! I watched him drag you in the mud." Arty points a finger at Janice and shoots me an open-mouthed scoff. "He Killed my parents!"

"No, he didn't kill your parents, or mine. He saved me— you know after he took us. He's… he's my boyfriend umm, consort," I reply tentatively with a weak laugh.

Both Nick and Arty stare me down. Arty plunges in with abandon, "He's your boyfriend? Really, you have a boyfriend? I was beginning to think you liked girls. Not that there's anything wrong with that. I don't even want to know what a consort is. Wait is that short for gigolo?" Arty holds his hands up while his face turns beet red.

Nick replies and shutters out a laugh. "As if you're one to talk, Arthur." For a second I couldn't tell if he was going to start crying again or not.

Janice cuts in, bristling, "I don't see how Sarinah's feeling toward me is any business of yours."

Nick releases a deep chuckle, only to be joined by Arty. It is contagious, and I begin to laugh too.

Janice returns a sickly smile and a dry mirthless laugh, which only brings on a new round of coughing, gasping, and laughter.

When we finally stop, I look to the portal, then back to the guys. "Do either of you want to go home?" I inquire.

The smile on all our faces fades like last year's tan. At the same time, Nick says no and Arty says yes.

I knew the answers before I asked.

Arty rushes on, "But I don't want to go right away. I'm looking for someone, a woman, a Fae named Pil." Arty smiles and dips his head, peering up at me over the top of his glasses.

Nick shoves his shoulder. "Man, are you still going on about her?" Nick rolls his eyes and head to look at me. Then coughs back an emotion before it can take over.

Arty replies, "Yes, she helped me. I would have lost it if it wasn't for her... and you. Can't a guy ask? Geez." Arty crosses his arms, placing his hands under his biceps.

I look from Nick to Arty and back. They both carry the same stance. I guess hard times make you closer. Shaking my head at them both, I reply, "I'll ask for her."

Arty continues by changing the conversation. "So, what's with the wings and horns? And how in the fuck do you sleep on those?" He pushes the crooked glasses back up his nose and the hair out of his eyes.

My mouth drops open, turning me into a guppy. Nick claps his hands together.

"Awe, Arty, I knew I liked you, man. Finally, someone who can make her shut up." He tilts his head up to the sky and closes his eyes, then presses his hands together in prayer. "Thank God, Sarah shut up." I smack him in his arm. He jumps back laughing.

"For your information, I haven't slept yet. I came looking for you." I punch Arty's shoulder. He rubs it. "Ouch, you got stronger. Look, I'll stay the night, but I want to go back in the morning. If you find Pil will you let me know?" He tilts his head down to hide most of his face.

I'd never known Arty to ask after any girl so I thrust my hand out. "It's a deal." We shake.

"Now that all you children have found each other, I've come to collect my son and kiss my granddaughter." My head whips around at the sound of Puca's voice.

Nick and I reply at once, "Son?"

"Granddaughter?" Then we look at each other. In unison, "Puca's your Dad/Grandfather?" Then, we turn and face Puca

Puca sighs. "You each think you're the only ones. I have been around a long time." His canary yellow eyes twinkle with glee while he smacks Nick on the back.

"Don't you ever wear a shirt?" I demand in an attempt to deflect my discomfort.

Puca shrugs. "Why should I hide such perfection? Come, children, the Queen needs rest and a safe place to do that. My home will suffice until she decides what she wants to do." He releases a belly laugh; not that he'd ever had a belly, more like a board attached to the place a belly should be.

I grumble, "You'll need to explain this one to me sometime. How many kids do you have?"

Puca smiles a big toothy grin, then leans in and whispers, "One of the great parts of being the first- and one-time king: I don't explain, anything, ever." He chuckles and opens a portal.

Janice takes my hand and leads me to Puca's portal, allowing me to step through ahead of him. I catch Arty's eye and he gives me a half smile and a thumbs up. His aura tells a different story— it's dingy brown, only flashes of color come through. The truth is, when he asked after Pil, I saw him, really saw him. He's in love.

CHAPTER 30

"And you're sure you don't know who and where Pil is?" Arty quietly demands.

I sigh. "Arty, if I knew anything I would tell you." I rub his arm.

He ducks his head as if to nod, but really to hide his haunted eyes. It is tearing me up inside. Arty has lost everything. Now he is even going to lose me. With my power, I can stop him, but I'd never be able to live with myself. His desolation wakes out from him.

When I step through the portal, the surreal feeling of Oz settles over me. All the houses in our old neighborhood sag with years of disrepair. The grass crisscrosses the road and walkways. Trees have grown up, cracking and breaking cement. The doors to most houses yawn as vacant openings, their windows empty of glass. Everywhere wakes of abandoned neglect.

Tall grass brushes the underside of my arms as I pick my way over the dry bones scattered over the road, moving to the sidewalk. Humming Itsy Bitsy Spider, I move webs out of my path, not willing to disturb the creatures' diligent work. I've learned a healthy respect for the miniature weavers of silk.

"Are you sure we're in the right place? This looks like the end of the world came and went. Only we missed it," Arty quips, then squeezes my hand.

I know he's trying to make a joke to lighten the mood. We both stop at the edge of my parents' property line. My hesitation mirrors his— neither of us wants to cross the invisible line humanity drew dividing his land from mine. Somewhere in the next three feet lay Arty's parents in their many parts. I can't recall whether Arty's dad was on the sidewalk or the grass but his head lay on the grassy parking strip. His mother had crumpled not far from his father's remains. The ache starts at the base of my tongue, working its way down my throat. Dry heat steals over my eyes.

"We can cross the street, we don't need to walk here," I entreat in soft tones for fear I might cry if I raise my voice even a bit.

He sniffs. "No, whatever is here it isn't them. They're gone… for a long time, I guess." His voice breaks on the last words.

I squeeze his hand again as he turns into me. I wrap my arms around him as he shakes with grief.

I swallow the lump back and push my own pain away. The grass wakes the outline of his parents' skeletons. My Fae eyes pick out the leftovers of their bodies and it only reinforces, I can never stay here. While humming under my breath, the soil pulls back, allowing whatever remains of their bodies to sink into the ground. Arty need never find them or see them.

Magic wakes out from us, blanketing the surrounding area for miles. The ground gapes open and swallows the remains of every body for miles. I didn't want Arty to live seeing the death Fae had left behind in our wake.

I'll take care of the rest of the world later.

Arty chokes out, "You didn't have to hide them. I know they're here, but thank you." He pulls out of my embrace, his black hair hanging in his face and over his shoulders. I push a lock behind his ear to reveal the face I'd never thought to live without. We both swallow.

"Do you want to see where Sorensen hid his secret room?" I inquire while cocking an eyebrow and throwing him a half smile.

Arty rubs his palms into his eyes and coughs, then places his cracked spectacles on his nose. "Yeah, it's all I've been thinking about since the shit hit the fan." He gives me a half smile while rolling his eyes.

Air moves over my shoulders as I try to hide my nervous excitement. Learning to control wings is not something I'd had on my bucket list.

"Maybe you should fold those away. I think the horns growing from your head will scare them enough." Arty waves his index finger at the gossamer wings on my back.

Taking a deep breath, I concentrate on the muscles along my spine, relaxing them, then swing my arms in an arc. They fold down flat against my back. I smile in satisfaction. *I can do this.*

We hurry down the street, ducking through the front door and making a beeline to the kitchen. I drag Arty behind me, coming to a dead stop in the middle of the room.

"Want to take a guess?" I prod breathlessly.

Arty huffs, strolling around the room. The back door is still in good order, the glass unbroken along with the windows to the kitchen.

"This must be the only house around with a pane of glass left," he remarks, opening the back door and allowing it to swing freely into the room. "It didn't make a sound. Reminds me of the grate on your dad's tunnel." Arty ceases pacing by the cabinet. The glass doors hang limply from wood chunks. The handles lay at his feet on the floor, and he nudges one to the side.

Though the glass on the floor gives the appearance of chaos, I know better.

"This isn't some Anne Frank thing, is it? Cause that would be dumb. Sorensen was smarter than that, wasn't he?" Arty inquires, then throws his hands up and grabs the side of the china cabinet wrenching it away from the wall.

"Are you fu—" Arty's words die on his lips.

The dark opening is filled by a single individual. A gray-haired man with a scraggly beard peers at us over the top of two barrels in the dark moonlight.

"Don't try any of your Fae tricks on me, they don't work. I'm a live-and-let-live person. If you leave, I'll let you live." My father's voice is cold and study. I don't know what I was expecting. I knew he wouldn't recognize me, but Arty, I'd been hopeful.

"I'm not here to play Fae tricks, only to return this man to his family," I reply. Arty and I agreed I would act as an unconcerned party. My dad didn't need to know I was now the Queen of Fae, or to see how I'd changed.

He swings the two black barrels my way, his watery blue eyes barely focusing on me through the heavy gray brows that ridge his forehead. Even with his face pressed to the sight, I can see how haggard he's become with deep lines running from the hollow of his cheekbones down to the jowls hanging from his chin. His gnarled fingers play over the gun's grip. The large shoulders I'd ridden upon as a child, always so strong, hung with muscles no longer locked around the bone.

"George, don't shoot us, please," Arty asks with both hands up.

I hum a protection bubble around Arty and turn to face my father, ignoring the ache pressing the back of my throat. "The war between humans and Fae is over, you have nothing to fear from me or any other Fae. Arthur requested we bring him home, to you." The ache in my chest grows. I'd rehearsed what I'd say over and over, hoping to sound aloof and emotionless. My voice comes out cold and uninterested. My insides chill with the certainty I will never see my father again. I want to run to him and cry in his arms, but Queens don't get the luxury of tears or hugs.

He can no longer see the daughter hidden by the Fae I've become. It's how humanity protects itself: by denying the painful truth.

"George, open your eyes; can't you see the forest for the trees? It's Arty. Now be thankful for what you have, don't pine away for what you've lost," my mother's sweet, sing-song words wake her love for me.

I smile down at her, pressing my lips together to hide the trembling. Her own blue eyes beam back at me.

My father's head whips back to Arty and rakes over him, only to raise his brows in surprise.

"Where is Sarah?" he demands. "She went back for you and you come back with that?" He pokes the gun barrel my way. "Where's my daughter, Arthur?" He lowers the barrel a fraction of an inch.

My throat tightens as my mother continues ignoring my father's cutting remarks. "Is Puca here? Did he come with you?" she directs her question at me while bobbing her head back and forth in an effort to see around mine and Arty's forms.

"No, I don't need him to travel," I give her my quavering reply, clearing my throat.

"George, take Arty downstairs while I talk to our guest." For once, my mother stands tall and strong. I've never seen her order my father around. But she did, and he lowers the shotgun, moving deeper into the gaping shadows of the stairwell with Arty trailing behind.

The shock of my father's aged appearance is nothing compared to my mother's, she's only aged a day. Her hair is still blond and glossy without a single strand of gray, while not one-line creeps around her eyes. She still carries the tone of youth in her muscles.

Her arms swing wide to encircle me. "It was the same for me when first I returned," she confides.

"You know me?" I whisper.

She waves my inquiry away. *How very Fae.* "Everyone I'd ever known was long dead and food for worms. Not even a cross or stone left to mark their passing when I returned. I cried and raged at Puca. He never explained the price of Fae or about the passing of time."

I push back, eyes wide. "When were you born?"

"The Year of Our Lord, 1306, May Day. I was thought to be a changeling. But my mother kept me anyway. They didn't in those days—changelings were left out in the open for God to take. Damelza, my mother, had a mind of her own. Always demanding her own way and finding a way to get it." She gave me a one-eyed wink, the way only someone with Fae blood could, never moving any other muscles.

My mother had never spoken of her family or her mother. She'd always said they died long ago. When she stares off into the distance I never dreamed of the truth in her words. I always thought my mother was the weak one. How wrong I was.

"You won," she states. "I always hoped you would. And Cernunnos?" She falters, her hand covering her mouth.

"He lives, I found another way. All of Fae needs to find another way to exist. I'll show them. Don't worry, I got this." She turns back to me as the smile dances across her face.

She nervously clasps both hands together. "Your crown suits you… can I see your wings?" my mother inquires.

I gasp.

"You think you're the first Queen of Fae I've ever met? I know what a fairy queen looks like, so show me." She keeps her hands locked together.

Stepping back, I open my wings enough to fill the room without taking out the overhead light fixture. The gossamer flesh reflects the moonlight as it trails from the windows. My wings give off their own green glow, matching the marking on my skin.

"You're beautiful, Sarinah! You can't stay, though. The sun will rise and you will burn with it, I know. Is Arty staying?" she inquires while biting her lip.

I lay my wings flat onto my back swallow and reply, "Yes, Arty said he'd stay and take care of you. I'll visit when I can." I gulp. The words stick in my throat, not wanting to leave my tongue. By the time I'm able to return they may all be dead. Pushing the fear away, I press my lips together and hold the anguish in check.

My mother slowly enunciates every word, saying, "I will still be here. I'm touched by Fae and don't age like humans. If you can't come, send Puca, he'll come for me. Don't be sad. This is how it was always going to be for me and you. We are Fae." She shrugs.

"What about Dad and Arty? They just die like every other human?" I retort.

"Yes, I'm sorry, sweetheart. That is the way of life. Your father would never survive in the Hallowed Hills, and I won't leave him. Arthur is welcome to return with you if he wishes. We can survive without him. I do have some magic and can protect us." My mother's admission isn't a shock. Her face twists in hurt. The lie she's lived has cost her. Her guilt from it wakes off of her, coloring her aura.

"I offered to stay." The deep timber reverberates around the room. "I need a break from Fae." Arty's matter-of-fact answer masks the truth of his broken heart.

His aura is colored deep brown with sadness. From the moment I'd found him in Deston's castle, he's been a joyless lovesick fool. His incessant inquiries into Pil only cement the truth.

My mother's eyes linger on Arty, assessing him in the all-too-familiar Fae fashion. I don't know why I hadn't noticed all the little similarities. It had been right in front of me the whole time.

"Why do you hate Fae so much?" my inquiry jumps out before I can check my tongue.

Her smile spreads across her unblemished face. "I don't hate Fae, I hate what they do. You think I hate them just because I wouldn't let you dress up as one or watch one of those ridiculous movies? They aren't the real Fae. As you can see, only pixies and Queen's have wings. Those stories would only have filled your head with lies and I couldn't tell you the truth." She fiddles with one of the broken teacups in the cabinet. "You wouldn't have believed me until you presented. I tried to teach you the magic when you were little, but you didn't take." The guilt reeks from her, battering the walls.

"You could have told her when they landed," Arty brakes in to defend me.

"Puca was supposed to come and take you and train you to keep you safe. We weren't supposed to leave the house. Your father had other ideas. I knew about the tunnel, but I didn't know it was finished. I never got a moment long enough to explain." She sounds weak and frightened.

"You were hiding from Jacques, weren't you?" I see it all so clear.

She nods her head—her eyes had grown to the size of the saucer she kept toying with.

Everyone has secrets. Even parents. My mom had been terrified Jacques or Deston would find me. All her cleaning had been her spreading as much magic as possible to hide us.

"Every time I read the papers telling of a changeling girl going missing nearby, I quaked. Jacques is more dangerous than a pit filled with vipers," she breathes out the whisper.

"All the challengers were part Fae?" Arty demands.

My mother turns her back on us, running her fingers across the wall as she walks to the far window. "Only a Fae could have won the challenge." She tentatively chances a glance over her shoulder. She turns with purposeful steps and stops short in front of me. "It is the past, let it go." She reaches for my hands. "Your father will be up in a moment to make sure I'm still breathing, so kiss me and say good-bye." She gives me a tight-lipped smile.

As I lean in to hug her, a myriad of questions storm through my mind. But breathing in the scent of honeysuckle and laundry soap quiets them. She rocks back and forth and thrust me away, then quietly skips down the stairs.

Arty moves between me and my mother's retreating steps. "Will you keep looking for Pil?" he pleads.

"Yes, I will, and I'll come and tell you if I find her. Are you sure you want to stay? I'm totally selfish and want you with me." I grab his hand with both of mine.

"I'd only be a third wheel—Janice doesn't want me hanging around all the time. In my heart I can't stand to look at the guy. I can't defend you, and Fae only respects its own. I would be nothing more than a pet in their eyes. I can't live like that. There's a laundry list of reasons I won't stay. The only reason to make me stay is missing." Arty replies. It's clearly killing him as much as me. He cups my cheek and kisses my forehead. "Take care of yourself, Dee."

I cough a laugh. "You too, Dumb." Then, I pull him into a hug and cling to him for a minute.

"I'll be back," I whisper.

"Of course, you will. Hopefully, I won't be too old by then." He cuffs me on the chin.

My eyes blur as I picture my chambers and thrust my hand out, creating the portal. My wings flutter, moving the dust around the room. Then, I step through the opening and watch as it slams shut. The magic wakes, moving away from its location.

My heart burns hot and cold as every door slams closed and the walls weep for me. Pulling in a deep breath, I turn and fling the doors to the throne room open, banging them against the walls. Janice stands on the other side. I go up on my tiptoe's and kiss him lingering for just a moment. Then turn to face the room.

There, on either side of the throne standing still as a statue, are Deston and Jacques waiting for me to free them from wild. But that will never happen. The power of the princes is broken.

Janice extends his hand and leads me to the stone throne. Flaring my wings to their full size, I lowered myself onto the cold, unforgiving seat.

The sea of Fae faces all curtsy and bow in obedience. Not a single human in sight.

No amount of magic can erase the carnage this room has held. I still see the bloody floor and dead bodies littered haphazardly in my mind's eye. Nikki's had lain just outside the door where she fell.

Nikki was part human and Fae. She used magic too, just not as well as I did. I could never think of Nikki without bringing Nick to mind.

Since the eruption of my wings and thorny crown, the pain has receded, but the memory remains. In order for a butterfly to take flight, it must fight its way from the chrysalis holding its wings hostage. I struggled to be freed from the bonds of my cocoon. I don't know if my humanity was my chrysalis or not, but my wings can take flight and so will I.

Janice leans over and whispers, "My queen, what is your bidding?" The scent of vetiver and spice moves with him.

"Present the first petitioner," I reply, heaving a sigh.

The female Fae bows low, and her long legs crossed as if she should've worn a dress and not the leather leggings. Her black and white hair trails down over the floor. She raises her head to reveal her bright orange eyes, and a body surrounded by the muddy brown aura of heartbreak.

"Your Majesty, I am Pil and I've come to beg a boon."

The end

Thanks for reading! I hope you enjoyed Twist of Fae.

Make sure to get your copy of the next installment of These

Hallowed Hills - Twist of Fae

Take a sneak peek of Twist of Fae.

TWIST OF FAE
CHAPTER 1

Humans think fairies are born from from a human child's first laugh. Ridiculous we are born like everything else, from magic.

Only a boon from our Queen, is capable of creation. The boon requires a favor, a task, or a quest and you must succeed.

I was created for a war.

Our Queen wanted a war so my father made one. She didn't want just any war, she wanted a great war that would dwarf all others. She wanted the humans to truly suffer. She wanted to see exactly how far they would go destroying each other.

So my father he tricked everyone into war. Not because they hated one another, although I'm sure they thought they did. Not for a perceived wrong, no. They went to war for no other reason than the simplest, they went to war for envy. It is a fae's favorite downfall. Because at our core we are all envious in our own way. We always desire what we cannot have. Many times we take what does not belong to us, we are Fae it is our way.

My father named me Pil after some ridiculous human idea, he said it amused him.

Then our Queen died she left us alone with only one mandate go to the human world and find another. Sounds like the simplest of tasks, I figured I would pop up and be done in a night. All we had to do was go and find a human with just a touch of fae blood. You coax the magic out of her, who wouldn't want to be a fairy.

Humans tell ridiculous stories, with their movies and drawings. Little teeny creatures flittering around on wings. Only a Queen has wings.

My mother Queen faded and finding a replacement was more difficult than we had anticipated. All the candidates had no idea what they were. Their human side clings to that world, to that ridiculous death and diseased world with no magic.

I stole a few girls for myself turned them over to my Lord and he in turn rewarded me. None of my choices survived I was not punished, none of us were. We trick and play, to control 'her'.

But that Queen too faded, so the cycle began again.

Questioning a Liege Lord is not forbidden, it's just not wise. To question is to challenge its an assumption that you know better or you're wiser somehow. I had no desire to challenge our Lord. I'm not capable of that kind of fight. I know what I am, a hunter nothing more nothing less. My whole existence is to serve my master. I can choose as much as any fae. But I was not born to rule, I was born to hunt and kill.

If you've enjoyed what you've read here please give it a little love and leave a review or feel free to follow me on Amazon Or send me an email slmason1889@gmail.com or follow me on Instagram @s.l.mason_author

For the most up to date information on the Killing Gods Universe or These Hallowed Hills visit:

Quickquillpublishing.com